UNRAVELED

GLUTTONY

7 DEADLY SINS
BOOK 2

HALEY RHOADES

Copyright © 2020 Haley Rhoades

All rights reserved.
Unraveled is a work of fiction. Names, characters, and incidents are all products of the authors imagination and are used fictitiously. Any resemblance to actual events or persons, living or dead, is entirely coincidental.

Any trademarks, service marks, product names, or named features are assumed to be the property of their respective owners and are used only for reference. There is no implied endorsement

Cover created by @germancreative on Fiverr

Created with Vellum

I dedicate this book to first responders, healthcare workers, retail staff, and small businesses.
The Covid-19 Pandemic of 2020 opened our eyes to the importance of each of you and your jobs.

Enhance Your Reading
Check out the **Trivia Page** at the end of the book
before reading Chapter #1.
No Spoilers—I promise.

Look at my Pinterest Boards for my inspirations for characters, recipes, and settings. (Link on following pages.)

Prefer your romance on the **sweeter** side?
Look for this story under my **PG-13** author name Brooklyn Bailey.
BrooklynBailey.com

PROLOGUE

I hate Las Vegas; I hate girls' trips. *How stupid must I be?*

"Let's fly to Vegas for two days. It'll be fun, just us girls shopping, eating, gambling, and dancing." I spoke those words. How innocent I thought their meaning to be.

Our other girls' trips were fun. We let loose, we partied, and we returned to Iowa prepared to resume our daily lives.

Not this time; not this trip. There's no returning to our normal, daily lives after last night. My life is forever changed.

A chance meeting led to two nights of dinners and clubs with a famous rock band. Most would say we were very lucky to spend our time with them. I can say I enjoyed every minute until the sun rose this morning.

Married. I had to ruin it by drinking too much, marrying a member of the band, spending the night with him in my bed, and not remembering a moment after the six of us enjoyed dinner.

It takes two to tango; I know. He claims he doesn't recall our trip to the wedding chapel or the night we shared, and I want to believe him. From the two days we've spent together, I feel I can trust him.

Married. Together for two days, and we wake on the third naked and married.

1

MONTANA

Three days earlier

"Thank you for forcing me to take a girls' trip," I murmur under my breath as we walk from the lobby through the casino of the New York, New York hotel.

"Just doing my best friend duties," she states, nudging my shoulder, as we stand at the bank of elevators. "My job is to force you to spread your wings and step out of your comfort zone, and you do your best to reign me in and keep me out of jail," she states as we ride the elevator to our floor.

"That's true." I allow her to step from the elevator with her two large, pink, rolling suitcases, before I exit with my one carry-on bag.

I seem to keep several things on my plate at all times, often forgetting to set them all aside and enjoy the day. I love that Peyton sees my weaknesses and helps me take a breath, take a chance, and enjoy life.

As she fumbles with her luggage and oversized purse, I quickly pull my room card from my pocket, swipe it, then throw the door open wide for her to enter. My breath catches as I take in our hotel room. I expected it would be like the tiny rooms on the cruise ships we've shared during trips with our families. I mean, you don't come to Vegas to spend most of your time in the hotel room. Ours, however, is larger than a typical hotel room; it's not quite a suite, but two full-sized beds are separated from a common area with a sofa and chairs. It looks like Peyton went all out in planning this girls' trip.

"I'm setting my timer for 45 minutes," I inform her as I place my makeup bag on the bathroom vanity. "Just a little time to relax and freshen up. We've got a lot of ground to cover on the strip and only three days here."

"Relax," she admonishes, scrolling through social media. "We're not on a schedule. We'll go with the flow and see what we see along the way. If we miss anything, we'll just have to come back at the end of summer."

I fear if she had her way, Peyton and I would travel every weekend. I pull a bottle of water from the mini fridge; the cold beverage washes away the heat of Las Vegas in May.

"Montana!" Peyton's high-pitched voice startles me from across the room. "Do you know how much they charge for water in the minibar?"

I turn, rolling my eyes. She knows that a six-dollar bottle of water is well within my means. I mean, I don't spend money frivolously; when I need something, I can afford it. I pull a second water bottle from the small refrigerator, tossing it onto the bed near my friend.

"What are you doing?" Peyton asks, eyes glued to her phone.

"I'm changing out of my comfy travel clothes into my knock-'em-dead-in-Las-Vegas clothes," I tease.

It's not really a knock-'em-dead outfit, more like a makes-me-feel-cute-and-sexy outfit. I'm pairing a silky, black with white polka dots tank top that hugs tight to my breasts and abdomen with a black miniskirt that ends mid-thigh and high-heeled, black sandals. The heels with the skirt place my long, toned legs in the spotlight. Peyton says my legs are my best asset. To finish the look, I secure my hair in a loose ponytail, with tendrils framing my face.

"How do I look?" I pretend to stroll down a catwalk, posing at the sofa where she sits, phone in hand.

"Holy hotness. You're pulling that out on our first night in town?" Her smile tells me she likes the look.

"I have other head-turning outfits for the next two nights," I inform her.

"How you fit everything into one small suitcase I'll never understand. And no, I don't want you to teach me," she states. "I think I'm wearing peach tonight."

"I love your peach sundress," I remind her. "Time's a-wastin'," I prod, taking away her phone.

She complains but hustles to change. I'm sure, in her mind, the sooner she changes, the sooner she'll have her cell phone back.

The sounds of video-slot machines fill the air as I follow Peyton onto the casino floor, and bright lights flicker as far as the eye can see. Butterflies spread their wings in my belly as my excitement increases. Although I know the general premise of slot machines, I'm not sure on the logistics, and I'm eager to learn.

"Walk slower," I beg Peyton, so I may observe people playing the games. Every few steps, I pause and watch as a person approaches a chair, places cash into a machine, then plays. *I guess it's that simple.*

"Ready to play?" Peyton plops into a high-back, black, leather seat, patting the machine next to her.

I take my seat, pull a twenty-dollar bill from my clutch, then slide it into the slot. The machine registers my money and bright lights flicker into action. I feel giddy; all the stories of people winning on such machines flash through my mind. It's the potential to win that creates the buzz in my veins. I'm a realist, though; I'm aware of the probability of me winning.

"If we win $500, I'll purchase tickets to the Thunder Down Under for us," Peyton giggles as the wheels on her machine spin and lights flash.

Instantly, I know full well if we do to attend, Peyton will make every attempt to become a prop in their performance. While she'd thoroughly enjoy it, I'd be mortified. I take a deep breath, realizing odds are we will not win at slots.

We move from machine to machine, inserting a twenty and cashing out with less than a dollar. When the allure of the bright lights and loud machines eventually wears off, we sidle up to the casino bar for a drink then make our way outside.

"Excuse me." Peyton approaches an older couple on the walkway between our hotel and the MGM. "Would you mind taking some photos of us?"

The wife smiles, nodding. Peyton and I hug tight and smile proudly with the New York, New York hotel skyline behind us. Next, we turn to pose with the Las Vegas Strip lights behind us. We thank the couple, offering to take a photo of them, then continue on.

At street level, near Caesars Palace, Peyton places her hands on both of my shoulders. Facing me, she states, "We're gonna play the fifty states game while we're here."

I lift an eyebrow, having not heard of this game without riding in a car, and looking at license plates.

"Our goal is to take a picture with a person from each of the fifty states." She pulls her phone from her pocket.

This seems like a complicated task, requiring initiated conversations with too many strangers.

"This is our list of the states in alphabetical order," she explains, holding her cell phone for me to see. "When we pose for the picture, we'll signal the number on the list with our hands. Number fifteen is Iowa, so one person will hold up one finger and the other will hold up five. Then, we'll know the photo was number 15 which means Iowa." She smiles proudly. "Then, later, I'll post them on Instagram, so everyone knows how we are progressing in our game."

Will anyone care? I think to myself. Peyton's obsession with social media consumes most of her day. She easily posts ten times more than I do daily.

"It's practice for my career in marketing," she claims.

I've learned over the years that it's easier to give in when she's wanting to take selfies than it is to fight her. That means I have fifty selfies in my future.

"I'll show you how easy it will be to do this." Peyton smiles then scans the surrounding walkway. Her target in sight, she struts towards a group of three guys.

"Go Titans," she says, pointing to the ball cap on the guy in the middle.

The three guys cheer, proud of their team.

"Are you from Tennessee?" she asks in her flirty voice.

"Yep," a dark-haired guy responds.

"My friend and I," she motions for me to join her, "we're playing a game in which we need to take a picture with someone from every state. Can we take a photo with you?"

They comply. Peyton directs me to take the photo, looking at her phone she announces Tennessee is number 42 on our list. She asks the guy on her right to hold up four fingers while she holds up two. I count to three out loud and snap several photos with my phone. Peyton thanks the men, making an excuse for us to move on rather than hang with the three of them for the night.

"One state down forty-nine to go," she smiles, wrapping her arm around mine as we step up onto the escalator that will take us down to the strip below. "Go ask that older couple where they are from," she orders.

I want to protest, but it's futile. Unlike the group she approached, this couple is not wearing anything to clue me in on where they might be from.

"Hi," I greet. "My friend and I are trying to take a picture with someone from all fifty states. Where are you from?"

"We live in Nebraska," the woman announces proudly.

"We're from Iowa," Peyton informs them. "Can we take a quick photo with you?"

The couple agrees, so Peyton poses between them as they hold up fingers for twenty-seven. We chat with them for a bit before continuing our walk.

Peyton's photos impede our progress down the strip. I take a photo now and then of the buildings while she takes photos of desirable men. I take a picture of the two of us in front of the Eiffel Tower at the Paris Hotel. Peyton takes selfies with an Elvis impersonator along with a hot security guard outside of Planet Hollywood.

"Peyton, I'm tired," I complain hours later.

"Just wait," she begs. "I want a selfie of the two of us in front of the fountains, then we'll head back."

"I'll agree to the selfie, but we are taking a cab back to our hotel. It's almost midnight, and that feels like two a.m. to our bodies with the time change."

"We can't take our fifty states photos in a taxi," she whines.

"We took twenty pics; that's enough for our first night," I state, hands on my hips.

She mumbles her complaint then agrees to the cab ride.

2

MONTANA

The next morning

I find myself in a dressing room at a shop near Planet Hollywood as Peyton tosses dress after dress over the door to me. She's on a mission to find me the perfect little black dress. She claims I need a new LBD for clubs tonight. I assure her I packed appropriate attire, but she won't have it.

"I refuse to try this one on," I inform her through the door, tossing the dress back at her. "You know I won't wear a strapless dress." Peyton is aware women constantly tugging up a strapless dress ranks high on my list of pet peeves.

I tilt my head in the full-length mirror, turning this way and that, admiring a simple black halter dress with a flowing skirt that ends mid-thigh.

"I kind of like this halter one," I tell her as I slip it over my head then pull on my own clothes. "I refuse to try on another dress," I state, emerging from the fitting room to find Peyton browsing a nearby rack.

"Where's the dress?"

"What dress?" I ask, walking to her.

"You said you like the halter dress," Peyton reminds me, pointing toward the dressing room. "Go get it. You need to wear it tonight."

"I told you I don't need a new dress; I packed one." I make my way toward the register, hoping she'll follow me to pay for her armful of clothes.

"It never hurts to have a new LBD," she informs me, plopping her shopping spree finds on the counter. "Go grab it, and I'll pay for it."

I love my friend, but sometimes, she's too bossy. "Let me think about it," I defer. "I may find a dress I fall in love with at the next store."

Peyton's distracted by the cash register. The sound of the clerk scanning the tags on her dress, shoes, and handbag is music to her ears; she loves shopping sprees.

After lunch, Peyton stops to play at a roulette table, so I sit at an empty slot machine nearby. The lady at the machine next to mine wishes me good luck as I feed it my money.

"Have you won yet today?" The older, blonde woman asks, pressing the spin button in front of her.

"This is my first gamble of the day," I explain. "My best friend and I spent the morning shopping along the Strip."

"Well, the last two people who sat at your machine lost over $200." Her hand pats my forearm. "It should be ready to hit for you." She crosses her fingers and waves them between us to bring me good luck.

Her smile is infectious. I watch during her next spin as her wide, blue eyes shimmer with the flashing lights in front of her. She rapidly claps her hands and bounces in her seat. She's a ball of energy. The first two rows of her game line up, matching perfectly. Her hands fly to her mouth in anticipation of the third wheel. I can't believe my eyes. She matches all three columns and rows.

"You won!" I cheer from her side.

"I won," she parrots, clapping. "I never win."

Together, we watch as gold coins fall from a pot at the top down to the bottom of the video screen, while simultaneously the amount of money she's won continues to climb in the center. It hits 100 dollars, spins past 200 dollars, and doesn't seem to want to stop.

I notice in small type at the bottom right corner of her machine it says, "Win $4,350." I can't speak, so I point at my discovery.

The woman leaps from her chair, preceding to hop up and down, clapping, eyes glued to her machine until she tugs me from my seat to hop with her. Adrenaline flows through my veins as if I was the winner. It's amazing to witness such a win. She seems like the perfect person to deserve such luck. A casino employee in black pants, a white, long-sleeved shirt, and black vest approaches and congratulates her.

"I must gather some information from you," the employee states, with pen and pad in hand. "Please fill out your name, address, and phone number. I also must see your state issued ID."

The woman takes the pen and notepad then looks to me, bewildered.

"Take a few deep breaths," I suggest, placing my arm around her shoulders.

She nods, breathes, then fills out the information with a trembling hand. A small crowd gathers behind us to witness the magic that is Las Vegas. It's one of the few places you can turn twenty dollars into over four thousand.

The employee informs her she must finish playing the eight dollars she has in the machine and heads to get a check from the cashier, promising to return soon.

We sit quietly, staring at our machines, wide smiles upon our faces.

"My name is Dawn," she informs me between her spins.

"I'm Montana. I can't believe you just won $4300," I giggle.

"I know, right?" She laughs. "My best friend forced me to take a weekend trip. She all but threw me out of my house, promising she'd take care of the kids for me."

"Sounds like your friend knew you needed it. I'm glad you won." I bet another dollar and fifty cents in my machine. "How old are your kids?"

"Oh, I have two adult sons. One is 26, the other 21," Dawn states, turning in her seat to face me and my machine. "I'm also guardian to my sister's six-month-old daughter."

"Sounds like you have your hands full. Your friend must be caring for the baby back home, then? It's nice you have help."

"Iowa's known for being kind and helpful," Dawn informs me.

"I'm from Des Moines, Iowa," I inform her, unable to believe the coincidence.

"No way!" Her voice raises an octave. "I live in Des Moines, too. You wouldn't happen to be single, would you?"

Her eyes widen, and her megawatt smile is hopeful. I wonder if her sons inherited her bubbly personality.

"Well?" she questions when I don't answer.

"Um..." I'm saved from answering when the casino employee returns.

She hands Dawn the check and a copy of the information slip she filled out. I busy myself playing on my slot machine while she instructs Dawn on the taxes for her winnings.

I'm down to three dollars, allowing me two more spins until I need to insert more money or move on to another spot. I press the repeat bet button and watch my machine spin to life. It emits unfamiliar sounds and purple flashing lights strobe along the sides of the video screen.

"Jackpot!" Dawn squeals near my ear. "You've won a jackpot!"

I look from her back to the video screen. A matching game appears. It instructs me to choose coins until I match three of the same color, then I win the jackpot of that color.

Dawn points to the four jackpot options on the very top of the screen. "The least you will win is $149.22," she points out.

My first choice reveals a green coin; looking up, I see the green jackpot is over 900 dollars. I'd love that. Next, I uncover a red coin with a matching jackpot of $252.98. I'd be ahead if I won that pot. After that, I reveal a blue coin then a green one.

"Choose a green one," Dawn orders as if I control what color I will pick next.

Unraveled

I hover my hand over one coin near the center then move to hover over another coin in the corner.

"Follow your first instinct," Dawn encourages.

I press my finger on the center coin. It's green. *It's green! I just won $915.72!*

Dawn leaps from her seat, wrapping her arms around my neck as I remain seated. "You did it!"

"I can't believe it," I whisper, my breath escaping me.

"I told you this machine was ready to hit," she reminds as she releases me.

We stare in amazement as the video machine continues to announce my win with loud noises and flashing lights. Eventually, it displays my grand total of the jackpot and deposits that amount with my remaining dollar-fifty in the machine.

"It's under $1200, so you can just cash out and redeem a ticket," Dawn informs me.

High on adrenaline, we walk together towards the redemption machine to cash my white slip of paper in for actual money.

"We should get a drink to celebrate," she suggests as I pocket my wad of cash in the front pocket of my shorts.

"Okay," I answer, causing her smile to grow wider.

With drinks in front of us, Dawn turns on her barstool to face me. "You never answered me. Are you single?"

I nod my head. "I don't seem to be as lucky in the dating world as I am at slot machines."

"We should exchange numbers, so we can get together when we're both back in Des Moines," she states.

I know that she really wants my number to set me up with one of her sons. As much as I love this exuberant new friend I've made at the slots, I don't think it would be wise to allow her to set me up on a blind date with her son.

"Let's take a selfie to post our winnings on social media," I suggest. "Crud." I freeze with my hand in my back pocket. "I left my phone in the room."

"Here; use mine," she offers with a smirk before she leans in for the photo.

"I'm posting on Facebook," she shares. "I'm typing 'winner, winner chicken dinner' with it. What's your Facebook name so I can tag you in it?"

This woman never stops. I'm sure she drives her grown sons crazy with her aggressive attempts to set them up. We exchange names, and she tags me on her photos on Facebook and Instagram.

"While your phone's out," I begin, "would you mind taking another picture together? My friend and I are attempting to take a photo with someone from all 50 states. We'd planned to use a selfie of us, but that would be cheating." She nods, and I continue. "If you'll hold up one finger, I'll hold up five since Iowa is number 15 on our list. And, I'll take the selfie." I strain to extend her phone one handed and press to take the photo. I pull my arm back, and we inspect the photo. It looks good with our bright smiles from our big wins.

"While you have my cell, text the photo to yourself." Dawn grins.

I see what she's really up to; she'll have my cell number to use to set me up. As I want a copy of the photo, I text it to my number.

"I should go find Peyton and share my news. What will you do next?"

"I'm heading to Chippendale's tonight," Dawn whispers, blushing. "I have front row tickets."

I shouldn't be surprised, but I am. For a moment, I try to imagine my mom attending such a show with front row seats. I want to bottle up some of Dawn's aura to carry with me.

"Catch ya later," Dawn says as she heads in the opposite direction through the casino from where I need to go.

I can't stop smiling; I'm not sure if it's Dawn or my winnings that cause it, and I don't care. I should ask Peyton to return to the store and

Unraveled

buy the halter dress with a portion of today's lucky win; that way, I'll make Peyton happy, too.

My right hand reaches for my cell phone to text her, only to find it's not in my back pocket. Then, I remember; I left it on my bed in the room. I make my way to the elevator bank.

3

MONTANA

Excitement from my win still pulsing in my veins, I press the elevator button, noting the numbers above each door are increasing instead of going down. Normally, I'd pull out my phone to check for emails and look at social media while I wait; I'm surprised I didn't notice it missing earlier.

Eventually, a ping signals the arrival of an elevator car. I enter, pressing floor 12, hoping the doors close before others join me. I hope to avoid the awkwardness that occurs when trapped with someone else; I almost always feel like I should strike up conversation to end the silence. I breathe a sigh of relief when the doors close, and I'm alone.

I round the corner from the elevators, heading down my hallway, hearing loud chatter in an open office. One woman sits behind a large, metal desk as staff in housekeeping uniforms chatter with timecards in their hands. I smile and wave as I continue walking by.

At our room, I scan my keycard, turn the handle, and push the door. KLUNK! It only moves an inch.

Who is in our room? There's not a cleaning cart in the hallway. How did someone get into our hotel room?

Through the crack of the slightly opened door, I speak into the room. "Hello?" With no reply, I try again. "Anyone inside?" Nothing.

No noise. "Um, hello? This is my room. Please come unlock the deadbolt." I wait a bit; still, I hear nothing, and no one comes to the door.

I walk back to the open door with staff inside.

"Um, excuse me. The deadbolt has locked me out of my room," I explain.

"That happens sometimes when leaving the room," a manager-type lady states, lifting a walkie talkie to her face. "Give me your room number, and I'll send maintenance to help you."

Great. I wish I had my phone to entertain myself while I wait.

Carson

As I step from the elevator car, I adjust the bill of my ball cap atop my head. I keep the bill low while on the casino floor so others might not recognize me. Now, on my floor, I adjust it.

I'm walking to my room, because I need a break from the guys. I love them, would do anything for them, but all of us together, letting loose... They get to be too much for me.

I can't wait to crash in my hotel room, throw back a few beers, and try to write some lyrics. It's time I remedy the emptiness of my notebook, for far too long now the blank pages haunt me. I hope a few hours of alone time will spark some creativity.

We record our next album in seven days, and I have yet to write a single lyric. My writer's block has resisted for over a year now. I should lock myself in my room, order room service, and write non-stop for the next forty-eight hours. If only it were that easy, but I can't force the creativity.

Thoughts on my empty notebook, I cut the corner, walking close to the wall. *Crap!* I stumble to the left.

"Oh, I'm sorry." I continue down the hallway, my mind racing. *Why is she sitting on the hall floor?* I slow my strides. *Is she hurt? Locked out?* I turn and hesitantly approach the woman sitting against the wall across from a closed hotel door.

"Um... Are you locked out of your room?" I ask.

"Yes..." her small voice answers.

"I'll walk with you to the front desk to get a new keycard," I offer.

"Thanks," she smiles sweetly.

Holy cow, the girl has dimples.

"That won't help; it's the deadbolt. It locked when housekeeping left our room. They called maintenance for me, so I'm just waiting." She quirks her mouth at one corner.

"Would you like company?" When she shrugs, I slide my back down the wall to sit near her. "How long have you been waiting?"

"Not long, maybe ten minutes," she shares. "I left my phone in the room, so..." She stares at her empty hands and wrists in front of her. "They have weird deadbolts here. I've never seen a metal bar stick out with a metal flap as a deadbolt before. I guess that metal plate can move without really being touched."

"I wondered what that protrusion was. I've nearly hit my head on it twice already," I chuckle. "I think I'm gonna get a beer from my room; can I bring one for you?"

There's her smile again, and I can't pull my eyes from the dimple on her cheek. *What is it about dimples?*

"Sure," she agrees. "I can walk with you."

"You'd better stay here," I offer, rising to my feet. "I'd hate for you to miss the maintenance person."

I mentally urge myself to saunter toward my room, sure her eyes are on me; I can't let her see I want to hurry back to my spot on the floor beside her. In my hotel room, I snag the six-pack and bottle opener from my mini fridge. Then, I try to keep my cool as I walk towards her.

"Just how long do you think we must wait out here?" she laughs at the six-pack in my hand.

"I'm always prepared," I reply, with as much charm as I can. "When did you get to Vegas?"

"Yesterday," she answers. "And you?"

"I've been here a few days now," I answer, suddenly realizing I haven't asked for her name. "I'm Carson," I say as I extend an open beer bottle.

"Oh, I'm… um…" she stammers a bit. "I'm Montana."

"Nice to meet you." I clink the neck of my bottle with hers. Suddenly, I can't think of anything to talk about. "I know what we can do."

"What?"

"Let's play the name game," I suggest nervously. "What you do is name a celebrity with my name, and I'll do the same with yours. First one that can't think of a name loses. I'll go first. Hannah Montana," I begin.

"Ah, I see; you have a secret Miley Cyrus crush?" she teases me.

"No, I don't. It's your turn," I urge.

"Carson Daly," she rattles off, pride upon her face.

"Joe Montana," I counter.

Next, she answers, "Johnny Carson."

Think. Think. C'mon, you can do this. Montana. Montana…

"Ready to accept defeat?" she jeers.

I notice we've both sped through our first drink, so I open a second beer, stalling for time. "You win." I pass her the open bottle and grab another for myself.

We continue to chat as minutes pass, and I lose all track of time.

"Are you here on business or pleasure?" she inquires.

"I'm here with a group of guys," I hedge, not knowing how much I should divulge. "We're blowing off some steam before we get back to work. How about you?"

4

MONTANA

"I'm here with my best friend, celebrating the end of our sophomore year of college," I share.

As we chat, I attempt to check him out without letting him know I'm doing so. *Why would such a cute guy sit on the hallway floor with me, considering all that Las Vegas offers?*

His deep, dark blue jeans are worn white and thin at the middle of his muscular thighs and each knee. My eyes want to stare at his biceps, tight beneath his black t-shirt, when they flex as he constantly adjusts his ball cap. There's something about him... Maybe it's his deep-set, brown eyes or dark scruff on his jaw. *Why does he look so familiar?*

"What type of work do you do?" I ask, attempting to keep our conversation flowing.

A crooked grin slides upon his mouth. "I'm a musician."

I tap my index finger on my lower lip. It's on the tip of my tongue. I feel it coming any second, and I'll remember. "No way!" Heat crawls up my neck and cheeks. "You're..." I fan my overheated face. "You're..." I attempt to quell the clog in my throat. "You're Carson Cavanaugh."

I turn to face him, my legs folded yoga-style between us, my beer bottles on the floor beside me.

Unraveled

He peers down both sides of the hall before his brown eyes crinkle at the side, and his tongue darts out to swipe his plump, lower lip. The motion temporarily stuns me.

"I knew you looked familiar! A musician... Phish! Yeah, you are a musician, a freaking talented and well-known musician," I babble.

Of all the hotels in Las Vegas, of all the floors in this hotel, Carson Cavanaugh's room is just down the hall from ours.

"Shouldn't you have a suite high in a tower somewhere?"

"Nah." He's suddenly enthralled with watching his fingers tear the label from his brown beer bottle. "We've been on a tour bus, crammed in like sardines; I need my space. The guys have their suite, but I like to get my own room to get away." His eyes peer up to me through his long, dark lashes. "Eighteen months on tour is plenty of time together."

"I bet. Even my best friend Peyton and I would not last on a bus for a year and a half," I agree.

"Well, we're here for five days before we head into the studio to record our next album," he shares.

"I bet it's hard to be incognito here."

"Cat's out of the bag now." He removes his ball cap and combs his fingers through his dark brown hair that falls to his jawline. "When the four of us are together, it's hard. On my own, I can usually make it through most of the day with no one recognizing me."

I try to suppress my growing excitement. "I'm sitting in a hotel hallway with one of the greatest lead guitarists on the planet." I shake my head at my lame attempt to play it cool.

"Nah," he argues.

"You know darn well *Communicable* is one of the hottest rock bands, and you know your fingers work those strings as many only wish they could."

"So, I take it you're a fan?" He smiles, stunning me for a moment.

"Maybe just a bit," I tease.

"Just a bit?" he counters. "Tell me, who's your favorite band, then."

I smile as I try to come up with a list to impress *the* Carson Cavanaugh. "As I'm an Iowa girl, I'm partial to ZipTie."

"Of course," he parrots.

"Then, Seether, Five Finger Death Punch, Nirvana, and Communicable."

His smirk tells me he's impressed by my rock knowledge. I'm sure, because he's famous, women pretend to be fans when they aren't. *Wow. I still can't believe I am sitting here drinking Carson Cavanaugh's beer.*

Carson

She's too good to be true. Her sexy dimples lure me closer; her conversation keeps me entertained, and her genuine love of music seals the deal. I definitely need to spend time with this goddess.

Words flow. Word after word flows through my mind.

ball of yarn, unbinds me, laughter crumbles my walls,
come undone, unravel me, you're the only one

Lyrics are back; she's cured my writer's block.

She nudges my shoulder, drawing me from the song forming in my head. A man in a work shirt and dark pants pushes his cart towards us. The front right wheel squeaks and shakes erratically.

"Thanks for coming," Montana greets politely. "I'm not sure how this happened."

"It happens from time to time," the man's gravelly voice responds. "We've even created this handy-dandy metal tool to unlock it with."

We stand, watching as he feeds a two-foot long strip of metal through the barely opened hotel door. He grumbles as he inserts it over and over toward the top of the door and attempts to slide it down to catch the metal flap. We hear a pop then the sound of a piece of metal hitting the tile floor below followed by his murmured curses.

The maintenance man rummages through each shelf of his cart. "I thought I had a spare here somewhere." He unclips the radio from his hip pocket and calls to a man on the other end for help. "He'll be here soon." And with that, he leaves us to wait in the hallway again.

"Take a seat," I encourage, as my back slides down the wall.

"Do you think it'll be another half-hour?" she asks, resigning herself to sit on the floor again.

"Tired of my company?" I tease.

"More like I'm tired of my bottom falling asleep." She wiggles and shifts into a comfortable position.

Much to my dismay, a maintenance person quickly approaches. He slips a metal piece through the door crack, pulls it back fast, and poof! The door swings open.

Montana

Still unbelieving, I search around our room, ensuring nothing is missing. I slide my cell phone into my back pocket, grab my debit card from my purse, and tuck it into my front pocket. I glance at the metal plate of the lock as I exit the room. Surely, it won't happen a second time.

"Oh, um..." I sputter, startled by the man standing in the hallway near my door. It's Carson. "What are you doing out here?" I look down the hall in both directions.

"I thought I should wait for you, so you wouldn't be walking alone." His mouth quirks up at one side.

His smile warms my belly. He's too damn sexy.

"I'm a big girl," I state as we move toward the elevators.

"I know," he responds. "I wouldn't want my sister walking alone through this large hotel or the casino, though."

"You shouldn't have," I argue.

"I wanted to," he informs, peering into my eyes while we wait on an elevator.

I search first his eyes then his face in its entirety. It seems he's not bluffing. *I can't believe Carson Cavanaugh of Communicable wants to spend time with me.*

While the elevator lowers floor by floor, I attempt to be discrete as I make sure I'm ready for a night in Las Vegas. My black, scoop-neck t-shirt remains wrinkle-free. With my left hand, I tuck it in on the side, allowing the rest to remain untucked and casual. I'm wearing my favorite white shorts with black platform sandals.

Peyton often rants at how muscular and long my legs look in these shoes. I glanced at my hair while in my room, unaware Carson waited for me mere feet away. I'm sure I pale in comparison to the Barbie-like beauties that congregate around him. *Oh well. No one knows me here, and I'll never see him again. I should make the best of it.*

5

MONTANA

Stepping from the elevator, Carson motions for me to walk toward the casino floor. His palm rests upon my lower back, just above my bottom; his heat nearly brands me.

"I should find Peyton near the tables," I explain.

"What?" He inquires, turning to face me.

The loud bells, whistles, and conversations of the casino surround us. In my heels, I don't have to stretch to speak near his ear.

"I need to find Peyton at the table games," I repeat, louder this time.

He nods, offering me his hand. Hand in his, he leads me through the slot machines. I'm awarded the opportunity to admire his tastefully snug jeans. *Oh, what an ass this man has.* His biker boots pound heavy on the floor while we cut our way through the busy casino as it comes to life for the evening.

When I bumped into him in the hallway as I left my room, I noticed he'd changed into a heather-gray, V-neck t-shirt with a navy and gray-plaid, button-down shirt over it. The buttons remain undone, and his sleeves are rolled up, allowing a hint of his forearms. They are tanned with a faint smattering of brown hair. He pauses abruptly, allowing me to admire the day's scruff highlighting his powerful jaw. The thought of the stubble scraping my most intimate parts creates the need to rub my thighs together.

"I'm texting the guys to meet us at the craps table," he informs before turning his eyes down to his phone screen. "Now, let's go find your friend."

Following behind him once more, I wonder if I am ready for him to meet Peyton, or better yet, for us to meet his band. I quicken my pace at Carson's side as we approach Peyton and her table. I wiggle my fingers a little, trying not to mess with any luck she might have. She waves me over then freezes, a wide smile upon her face at the sight of the Adonis walking beside me. She promptly cashes out her money.

"Who do we have here?" Peyton's wide eyes match her wide smile.

"Um…" I falter, not knowing if he wants me to introduce him or let him remain anonymous.

He extends his right arm. "I'm Carson." He pours on the charm, complete with his sexy smile. "You must be Peyton."

My wide-eyed friend looks to me, waggling her eyebrows; as he's standing beside me, he sees it all.

"So," she moves her index finger between Carson and me, "the two of you know each other how?"

We look at each other. "It's kind of a funny story," I begin. "I left my phone in our room, so I went up to grab it. Our deadbolt locked itself, and I waited in the hallway for someone to come unlock it."

"I nearly stepped on her. She was sitting on the floor near the wall, and I wasn't watching where I was going." He shrugs as if this thing happens all the time.

"So, you bumped into each other?" she inquires, not impressed with our chance meeting.

I smile, knowing my friend is about to owe me favors for the rest of her life; she'll flip when she learns who Carson is and that his band is joining us. Although she's not the metal head I am, she doesn't complain when I play their songs or attend concerts. Hanging around famous rockers tonight will cause her to lose her mind.

"Well, well, well, what do we have here?" A lanky guy in kelly green skinny jeans and a white Magnum P.I. shirt approaches Carson. "Where did you find two such lovely ladies?" he sing-songs.

"Eli, this is Montana and her best friend, Peyton." Carson pats his band mate on the back. "Ladies, this is Eli Patrick."

Eli looks like Shaggy from *Scooby Doo* with Paul Walker's blue eyes. His arms sport chorded muscles from years of banging his drum kit. Long, curly, light brown hair framing his face and deep dimples in his cheeks when he smiles in my direction only up his adorable factor.

I wave. Noticing the rest of the band a few feet behind him, I raise my chin, signaling for Carson to turn around.

"The party can officially start now," the lead singer announces, throwing an arm over Eli and Carson's shoulders.

I pay no attention to Carson as he makes introductions. I know each member from TV award shows and entertainment sites.

Warner Bradshaw, the bad-boy lead singer, wears black from head to toe. His skin-tight jeans, boots, and V-neck t-shirt are his trademark attire. A thick, gold chain around his neck draws my eyes toward the dark chest hair peeking out. I've often thought of him as a Jason Momoa look-alike. Although he's not as bulky in stature, his long, highlighted hair and large forehead resemble the star. His look is never complete without his tousled brown waves touching his shoulders, the mirrored shades, whether inside or out, and a sucker in his mouth. Gossip sites claim the sucker is always red and cherry flavored, as it has something to do with his childhood. It's not something I gave much thought to until now. *I mean, what grown man enjoys suckers in public?*

Flanking him is the quietest member of the band with the infamous, smoldering stare. Jake Johnson, the bass player, gives off powerful don't-engage-with-me vibes. I'm surprised as his looks are even more potent in person. His bright blue eyes are like Eli's. It states in his bio that his eyes are blue; I know that for sure. They've never looked this blue through a camera; maybe he wears contacts to cause a more dramatic contrast. His dark complexion and sandy, blonde hair might make you think of a surfer if he wasn't so stoic. He's not overweight but not as skinny as Warner and Eli. He is a big guy that works out, as if he needed to look even more intimidating.

"You did good," Peyton murmurs near my ear, drawing me back to the group conversation. "I call dibs on the guy in black."

I open my mouth to inform her there are two men dressed in black, but her knowing smirk and wink tell me she's claiming both of them. This should be an entertaining night.

6

CARSON

After introductions, Warner demands we hang at the MGM Grand before we do anything else. He's the stereotypical diva that goes with being a lead singer; he must always get his way. He promised some drunk millionaire last night that he'd return to play poker tonight, so we head across the street.

Montana and I hang to the back of the group while her friend seems at home, entertaining the rest of the guys.

"We'll give him an hour or two tops," I promise. "And, we don't have to stay with him at the poker table. There's plenty to do and see in the MGM."

She nods. "Would you mind taking a photo with me with the Las Vegas strip behind us?"

"Jake," I holler to the rest of the group, walking across the pedestrian bridge, "the girls need a pic."

Peyton bounces to Montana's side. They murmur for a moment before Peyton backs up, camera ready to take a photo. I wrap my arm around Montana's shoulders, pulling her tight to me as Vegas sprawls out behind us. Eli stands behind Peyton, teasing us, trying to crack us up as Peyton attempts to take the typical Vegas picture. She snaps several, and when she lowers her phone, Eli orders all of us to pose with the girls.

"Excuse me." Eli approaches a young couple. "Would you mind taking a couple of photos of us?"

I fear this couple may figure out who we are and post to social media, then, crowds of fans and paparazzi will swarm us all night. The female instructs us to squeeze together before she snaps photos with Eli's phone. When thanked, they continue on their way without incident.

"I'll wait until later tonight to post it," Eli tells me as we resume our walk toward MGM.

Our band manager ordered us to post on all of our social media platforms each day during our stay. Everything we do advertises our band; she's spreading the news about our new album every chance she gets. Fans know we are in Vegas; several seem to find us each night, but for the most part, they leave us alone.

As we enter the hotel, I lean toward Montana. "Why'd you hold up five fingers in our photo?"

She proceeds to tell me about their 50 states challenge, and the five represents California as the fifth state on her list. Interesting. It sounds like a fun game to play in one of the busiest cities in the world. Since she didn't ask, I assume, as a true fan of Communicable, she knows from my bio that I live in California.

At the edge of the casino, we split into two groups. Warner and Jake head for the high-limit poker tables while the rest of us venture further into the casino.

"What shall we play first?" Eli asks the girls.

"Crap!" Montana blurts, turning to face Peyton. "I forgot I was coming to tell you something when I realized I left my phone in the room." She scans the casino, pointing to a bar near one edge. "Let's go in there; we'll order a drink, and I'll tell you."

I'm anxious to hear what she has to say. I wonder if it's something she told me in the hotel hallway. I doubt that it is; nothing stands out as something she'd need to tell Peyton.

The ladies climb to sit at a high-top table with Eli's assistance while

I place a drink order at the bar. As soon as my ass hits the chair, she begins.

"I won $950 at slots today," she cheers, clapping her hands in front of her chest.

"Uh-huh," Peyton responds, her eyebrows raised and mouth open.

"I did. Here, I'll prove it."

Our drinks arrive, but we do not drink. We all watch as Montana opens her phone and searches for a photo. She scrolls through Instagram and pauses on a post of her holding her voucher of over $900. She reads the comments and hashtags a woman named Dawn posted.

"I didn't have my phone, so the lady next to me took the photo and tagged me. She won more than I did. Oh, and she's from Des Moines. Can you believe that?" With a few more swipes, she displays a photo in her text messages, marking Iowa off of their state game.

We pass her phone around, witnessing the amount on the machine and the celebration photo afterwards. Sure enough, she won nearly a thousand dollars.

"I can't believe you." Peyton pushes Montana's shoulder. "You always win. She's the luckiest person in the world." With her drink near her lips, she adds, "I mean she met you in a hotel hallway; she has to be lucky."

I smile at Montana, her eyes move to mine across the small, square table. She doesn't deny her friend's statement. She simply shrugs.

"The lady's name is Dawn; she's so sweet and perky. She's…" Montana searches for words. "She's sunshine, and she's contagious. She even tricked me into giving her my phone number to set me up with one of her single sons."

"Did you give it to her?" The words leave my mouth before I can stop them. *Way to play it cool, dummy.*

"She texted me our Iowa photo, so yes, she has my number. I'll just evade her attempts at setting me up on a blind date like I do my mom's."

Her eyes remain on me as she answers. *Play it cool. Play it cool. Don't let her know jealousy filled you at just the thought of her dating another guy.*

"Drinks are on you tonight," Peyton informs her friend.

"No," Eli and I state in unison, causing the girls to laugh.

"Chivalry is not dead," Peyton says. "Hey, give me your phone; I want to see that post again."

Peyton looks at Montana's winning photo, taps her finger once then scrolls several times. I can't help but wonder what she's up to. Suddenly, she stops scrolling, her eyes widen, and her jaw drops. She slides the cell phone across the table to Montana.

"I think you should reconsider letting her set you up with her sons. They. Are. Hot." Peyton points at the screen in Montana's hand. "It doesn't matter which one she sets you up with; they're all mega hot. Tell her you want to make it a double date. I want one of them." Peyton waggles her eyebrows, and Montana swats at her.

An anvil sits in the bottom of my stomach; I force myself to inhale a long, slow breath. *Why am I so bothered by a woman I just met being set up with another guy?* It's irrational, but I can't control the jealousy I feel.

7

CARSON

A commotion in the far corner of the bar draws my attention. A DJ sets up his gear, preparing to entertain the growing crowd. The overhead music pauses for a moment, then the DJ starts his first song. It's no surprise it's country; the decor of the entire place screams wood, cowboy, and country. Patrons around the bar begin moving to the music and singing along.

"The two of you should feel right at home," Eli states, pointing towards the DJ booth.

"Not everyone in Iowa farms and loves country music," Peyton snaps, clearly offended by his assumption.

"What's the line in The Beach Boys' Song?" Eli presses his luck. "Midwest farmers'..."

"Finish that statement and I'll demonstrate a city girl, kicking your ass." Peyton raises one perfectly shaped eyebrow in challenge.

Montana bites her lips, trying not to laugh.

"I'm sorry," Eli lies. "I didn't mean to tease you."

Eli loves to tease everyone. The more you demonstrate it bothers you, the more he teases.

"We do go to Beer Can Alley sometimes with friends, but country is not our jam," Peyton informs us.

"What is your jam?" Eli smirks at me before returning his gaze to Peyton.

"Pink, Avril Levine, and Maroon 5," Peyton answers proudly.

Eli raises an eyebrow at me. I gesture in Montana's direction, urging him to ask her.

She holds her palm in front of his face. "I've already been interrogated and passed with flying colors." She lowers her hand, smiling at me.

Eli's brow furrows as he tries to understand what she means.

Peyton rescues him. "She's a metal head. She loves alt rock, metal, grunge, and vintage. She drags me to concerts with her. After the last ZipTie concert, it took three days before my ears stopped ringing."

"I approve," Eli says to Montana then looks at me.

"I love this song," Peyton states, and Montana nods. "They play it on pop stations, too."

"So, you do listen to country," Eli states, smirking.

"You can't totally escape the genre when you live in Iowa," Montana explains. "We know the most popular country songs. Heck, we've even performed dance routines to them."

Dance routines? There's a new tidbit of knowledge.

"Tell me more," Eli prompts, leaning his chin on his hands, elbows on the table.

"We won the talent show at the Iowa State Fair when we were 17," Peyton brags while Montana gives her a death stare. "It's a huge accomplishment. The Iowa State Fair is a big deal; it's considered one of the best in the United States."

"So, the two of you," Eli seeks clarification, pointing between them, "did a dance routine on stage at the state fair?"

"I'll tell you everything, but you have to pinky-promise you won't tease us about it." Montana looks from me to Eli and back.

"Pinky-promise?" Eli furrows his brow.

Montana extends her pinky across the table to me as Peyton does the same toward Eli.

"Wrap your pinky with mine," Peyton instructs. "Now, promise you won't tease us."

Eli and I promise, trying to refrain from laughter. It's my first pinky-promise, and I want to keep it for Montana.

"We took lessons at the same dance studio for years. We entered the talent show twice in the under 18 category." Montana's eyes remain on her hands on the table in front of her as she continues. "When we were 17, our routine was a clogging dance to the Charlie Daniels Band hit *The Devil Went Down to Georgia*."

She takes a sip of her beer. "During rehearsals, those in charge decided our act would be more appropriate in the adult category. At the time, we didn't think that was fair, but we went ahead with it." She lifts her eyes to mine. "We were so good, we won."

"She's down playing it," Peyton states. "We were on fire, and the crowd absolutely loved us."

I squint my eyes, searching Montana's face for clues. She doesn't seem overly proud of it like Peyton. Maybe she's embarrassed; I can't quite read her.

"What were your costumes?" Eli seeks more details.

"We wore cut-off jean shorts, cowboy boots, a red and white checked shirt that tied at our waist, and cowboy hats." Peyton raises one eyebrow at Eli, daring him to comment.

"They weren't Daisy Dukes. My mom made sure the shorts weren't too short and that our bellies were covered," Montana clarifies.

"In my mind, they will be Daisy Dukes and a midriff top," Eli informs the ladies.

"You pinky-promised not to tease," Montana reminds him.

Eli mimics zipping his lips and throwing a key over his shoulder.

"So, the two of you must be excellent dancers," I mention. "What forms of dance can you do?"

"We took tap, jazz, and hip-hop classes," Peyton answers. "We also know how to two-step and line dance."

I nod. I'm such a moron; all I can do is nod. Words escape me. My mind's too busy imagining Montana dancing with me.

"Show us," Eli orders, pointing to the dance floor where a few couples are.

"Um," Montana hedges, "it's hard to dance to country in high-heeled sandals." She shrugs apologetically.

Eli purses his lips.

"We can show you a video of our performance." When Peyton suggests this, Montana freezes.

Eli and I lean our heads together to watch a short clip of their state fair performance. They weren't just good; they were awesome. They worked the crowd while moving in perfect unison. I pass the phone back to Peyton.

"I need to tinkle," Peyton blurts, climbing down from her stool.

Montana joins her without a word. *Why do girls do this? What's so special about joining each other in the restroom?* My parents have told me a million times not to try to understand the mysteries of women. Just accept it and go with it.

With the women out of ear shot, Eli leans closer to me. "I gotta see them dance."

I agree whole-heartedly. Everything about Montana intrigues me. I want to see it all and learn everything about her.

"I'll be back in a minute," Eli says, leaving me alone at the table.

I signal the waitress for another round of drinks then stare off into the distance, my thoughts on Montana.

Eli returns with shopping bags before the girls get back from the bathroom.

"What's in the bags?" I ask, then think better of it. Knowing Eli, I may not want to know.

"I told you I've got to see them dance," Eli reminds me. "Since sandals won't work..." His hand emerges from a shopping bag with new cowboy boots, or more correctly, cowgirl boots. "Now, they'll have no excuse. We'll request the Charlie Daniels Band then sit back and enjoy."

Eli's face shows he's proud of himself. I hope the ladies don't beat him to death with the boots. Speaking of the girls, they emerge from the restroom, crossing the bar towards us.

Carson

Sliding back onto her barstool, Montana thanks us for ordering another round, noting glasses of water are now on our table.

"What's in the bags?" Peyton asks, eyes glued to the large bags at Eli's feet.

He dips his hands into one oversized sack, handing red cowboy boots to Peyton. From the other bag, he passes brown boots with jade embellishments to Montana.

"Did I guess the right size?" he inquires.

Montana nods, and Peyton speaks, "How'd you know our shoe sizes?" Her nose crinkles and brow furrows.

"I'm not a stalker and don't have a foot fetish," he vows. "I've got small feet for a guy, so I often compare mine to women's. I figured Montana's feet were my size, and Peyton, yours look a little smaller. It's one of my many gifts," he brags.

"So, why did you buy us boots?" Montana inquires, her head tilted to one side, eyes like lasers on Eli.

"I dare you to perform your state fair winning routine," he smirks back at her. "You mentioned you can't dance in the sandals, so I found you boots."

Montana shakes her head. "You didn't just find us boots; you bought us boots. And, I can tell these are expensive, too."

"Don't mind her," Peyton urges, patting Eli's arm. "I absolutely love them."

"So, you'll dance?" He asks, face lighting up with the possibility.

"Um…" Montana hops back into the conversation. "New boots give blisters, especially without socks,"

Clearly, she has no intention of dancing for Eli.

"Ah…" he quickly responds, pulling another item from the bag. "I have socks." He waggles his eyebrows at each of them. "I dare you to dance. Do you accept my challenge?"

Peyton immediately nods her head. She folds her hands together and flutters her blonde eyelashes at Montana with pouty, pink-painted lips.

Arms crossed over her chest, she slowly shakes her head, a wide, closed-mouth smile growing on her face. I stare as her dimples slowly form in her cheeks.

"I'll need two shots." She holds her two fingers towards Eli's face. "And, time to get ready," she concedes.

Eli and Peyton practically float to the ceiling in their excitement. I smile, anxious to watch Montana move.

Eli is quick to fetch two rounds of shots. After the four of us take the first tequila shot, chasing it with lime, Eli disappears. Through the dark bar, I see his silhouette at the DJ stand. He's a man on a mission.

Peyton and Montana exit their barstools, Peyton snags one of the bags, and they return to the ladies' room with boots in their arms.

I'm alone for only a moment before Warner and Jake show up.

"Drinking heavy tonight?" Warner teases, slapping me on the back, harder than necessary.

"You can thank me now," Eli gloats in a raised voice, returning to the table. "Montana and Peyton are performing a dance for us in a couple of minutes."

Warner thanks him, wrapping his arm around his shoulders. Jake's blue eyes squint in my direction. I've often thought of him as an empath. As if his thoughts aren't enough to brood over, he takes on all of ours, too. I try to let him know I'm okay with Eli's plan.

Eli catches the others up on what we've learned about the girls, that they won the adult dance competition at the Iowa State Fair. He brags that we saw a short clip, and it was hot.

"Eli," I interrupt, "you did hear them say they were seventeen in the video, right? That's jailbait."

"Please tell me they're eighteen now," Warner groans.

"They just finished their sophomore year of college," I inform the group.

Based on Warner's relief at my answer, I assume he has plans for Peyton.

Montana

"I'm gonna kill you for this," I hiss toward Peyton.

Her reflection smiles back at me apologetically. I turn around, lean on the bathroom sink, and remove my sandals. I must admit my feet will be relieved to be out of my heels. I pull on one long black sock, then the gorgeous jade embellished boot. Eli certainly spared no expense and has fabulous taste. The chocolate ostrich contrasts beautifully with the jade tones. I tuck the sock a bit lower on my calf, so it's not visible before repeating the process on my right foot.

"It's like Eli knows me. I mean *really* knows me," Peyton declares. "These red booties are perfect. They're soft, maybe calfskin. I mean I'd buy something like them. Wouldn't I?"

I nod even though I know her boots are way over her price range. I can't believe Eli bought two pairs of expensive boots on a whim. I hope he gets his money's worth watching us. I shudder; I hope he doesn't get his rocks off on this. That would be too creepy.

"Ready?" Peyton asks me.

"No," I state honestly.

"C'mon," she tugs on my arm. "Can you believe we're hanging out with a famous rock band?"

We giggle. She's right; we're here to have fun, and so far, tonight has been more than fun.

Reentering the bar, I halt, and Peyton does, too. Warner and Jake are at our table. I don't want to go over there with the entire band present. Leaning towards her ear, I tell Peyton to go borrow a hat. I stride toward the bar.

"What can I get you?" the bartender greets while drying a glass.

"I realize this goes against cowboy code, but could I borrow your Stetson for a bit?"

Clearly, it's the last thing he expected to come from my mouth. His dark eyes assess me for a moment.

"I'll be the only one to wear it. And trust me, you'll be glad you loaned it to me."

With that encouragement, he places his hand on the top and transfers his black cowboy hat onto my head.

I turn on my boot heel, throw a little wave toward the band's table, and make my way to the DJ booth.

"You must be the dancer," he yells over the music. I assume Eli's already talked to him. "I'll put your song on after this one." I nod then search the suddenly crowded bar for Peyton.

When she seems to apparate by my side, I jump. She tips the bill of her hat to the guys occupying our table; Peyton's always performing, flirting, and working the room. I only turn my performance on for one song then flip back to the real me. The current song fades, and I pull Peyton with me to the center of the dance floor.

"Hey, ya'll," the DJ draws out in a fake country twang. "We are in for a unique surprise tonight. A dude approached me moments ago, telling me about a dare he issued to the two pretty ladies currently standing in the center of the dance floor."

A small spotlight focuses on the two of us while a few other dancers quickly exit the dance floor.

"These are Iowa girls, and they won the Iowa State Fair talent show. They will be sharing that performance with us tonight."

The patrons clap and cheer loudly; the air crackles with their excitement. I nod to the DJ, and we assume our first pose to catcalls and whistles.

8

CARSON

I grind my teeth, watching Montana lean towards the male bartender to chat. When he places his hat on her head, I feel my hackles rise. *I only met her hours ago. How can I feel this strongly for her? What is it about this woman that calls to every part of me?* I feel protective of her; I feel close to her. I feel like we're a couple—she's mine.

Taking a pull of my beer, I return to the present. The two girls stand in the center of the otherwise empty dance floor. The DJ stops talking as the song begins. As a guitarist, I can admit Daniels is a genius with the fiddle in his hands.

Montana smiles non-stop, her hands on her hips, her thighs and calves flexing with her movements. The sound of their boots on the wooden floor adds to the percussion. They're not really clogging or tap dancing as I expected. It's a routine to a country song with an occasional boot stomp.

They dance in unison until the lyrics reach the part that the bet is made. Now, Montana performs steps, challenging Peyton to keep up. They feed off of each other and the crowd's enthusiasm. While their steps grow faster and more complicated, their smiles never waiver. They command the stage, drawing every eye to them.

They end, bottoms leaning into each other, backs arched provocatively, with heads against each other and cowboy hats spinning on their index fingers.

The ladies bow as the gathered crowd awards them vocally and applauds. Peyton raises her palm, and Montana gives her a high five; then, the girls leave the dance floor. My eyes follow Montana as she heads for the bar. She leans over the bar top. The male bartender is more than eager to lean towards her. She removes the borrowed hat, placing it on top of his head. Before she pulls away, he places a kiss on her cheek.

I growl. It's a real, feral growl, and I'm grateful country music blares through the space to cover my reaction.

Montana

I can't wash the huge smile from my face, and there's an extra swing in my hips as I walk towards the band's table. Peyton's already there. Everyone's attention is glued on her, except Carson's. His eyes scan me head-to-toe multiple times as I approach.

He extends a fresh beer to me. When I grasp it, he pulls me tight to his side before I can take a sip.

"I owe Eli huge for talking the two of you into dancing," he murmurs huskily near my ear. There's a sexy smirk upon his face; when his tongue darts out to wet his lower lip, heat floods my belly. "I should have recorded it to watch over and over again."

I playfully tap his forehead. "Guess you'll have to rely on your spank-bank material up here." I look up at him through my lashes. His whiskey-brown eyes turn liquid.

The rest of the band turns their attention on us. Eli wraps his arm around my shoulders. "You didn't disappoint."

"Oh, we never disappoint in anything we do," Peyton claims, her eyes moving to Warner.

She's definitely pulling out all of the stops to make Warner aware she's up for anything. She seems to flirt with Jake almost as much as she does Warner. I pray she doesn't start a fight.

Carson

After hearing my bandmates mention hunger a couple of times, I text our band manager, Meredith, to see what she has set up for dinner.

Immediately, she responds, saying reservations are set for eight p.m. at Nobu in Caesars, and the limo is currently waiting outside the casino.

As the ladies climb in the black, stretch Hummer, the guys comment as they always do to the women they meet.

"Enough," I admonish them. "Remember your manners; Montana and Peyton are not groupies."

Testosterone rises within me, and I'm a little scared. *Why me? How can I have such strong feelings in so little time?*

Sensing my affections towards Montana, my band mates start to tease me.

Peyton sits between Jake and Warner toward the front. Montana sits between Jake and Eli. When I motion for Eli to move, he refuses. Just like in the cartoons, steam fills my head. I decide to sit on Eli's lap, knowing soon enough he will move over. My bottom only on his thighs, I don't lean back, and can't get comfortable. I look beside me to find Montana biting her lips at our antics.

"I think something's popping up," Eli declares.

I hop from his lap, banging my head on the ceiling. "Move," I demand. I'm not sure if it's my tone or my face that causes him to move. But when he does, I take a seat next to Montana.

Montana

"Stay here I'll be right back," Carson directs before walking to the hostess stand.

I note Carson stands close and addresses a woman holding an open iPad in front of her. In her navy pencil skirt, white silk blouse, and stiletto heels, she puts off an "I'm important" vibe to those around her. Her dark bra shows through her thin blouse with its top two buttons undone.

While he speaks to her, glancing at the screen, his hands remain in his front jeans pockets. Carson remains at the hostess station as the woman approaches our group. I look to the rest of the band, trying to judge their reaction to her.

"They've made the private room available," she speaks to the remaining three band members without acknowledging Peyton or me. "Join Carson, and they will take you to your table."

I waste no time grasping Peyton's hand and walking toward Carson. Behind me, I can faintly hear the conversation continue.

"Carson's in charge tonight. I have a meeting I can't miss." Her female voice is stern. "Let's not have a repeat of last night."

"Our table's ready," Carson announces upon my arrival at his side. "Guys, c'mon." He signals, swinging his arm.

We follow a gentleman in his mid-thirties toward the rear of the restaurant. I struggle to follow Carson through the dimly lit environment, so I grab the hem of his shirt with one hand. We're led to a private room through ornate sliding doors. In the center of the floor is a large table sitting two feet off the floor, surrounded by pillows. The thought of the band sitting on these pillows causes me to smile. This might be fun.

"May I take your drink orders while you look at the menu?" the host asks.

Warner wastes no time. "Two bottles of top-shelf vodka, a bottle of your best red wine, and a bottle of Jack Daniels."

Mentally, I attempt to figure if we really need that much alcohol. I'll only have a glass or two of wine; I don't want to forget a moment of my time with Carson and the band.

When the waitstaff delivers our drinks, Warner orders, "Oysters with Nobu Sauce, New Style Sashimi, oyster shooters, Rock Shrimp Tempura, Squid Pasta, spicy crab, Shrimp and Lobster with Spicy Lemon Sauce, brick oven-roasted lobster, scallops with jalapeno salsa, Hamachi Kama, crispy Shishito peppers, Kushi Yaki, chicken and shrimp, Nobu caviar tacos, and tuna tacos."

"Sir, if I might suggest," a waiter interrupts, "perhaps you'd like to order the tasting menu?" He points to the bottom of the menu. "For the entire table."

Warner nods to the man.

My eyes fly to the bottom of the menu in front of me. I nearly choke, finding it reads $200 per person. *It's $200 per person. That's $1200 for the food and doesn't include the drinks.* I take in a long, deep breath, then let it go slowly as I pass my menu along with the others to Carson on my right.

His eyes squint, and he mouths, "Are you okay?"

I nod and paste a smile on my face. I'm not sure how I feel about him paying over $200 for my meal. Make that over $400, as Peyton is here because of me. When we get a quiet moment, I'll need to offer to pay for my part.

I sit in awe at the amount of food and drink brought to our table. I scan the many serving dishes covering the entire top; there's no way we could possibly eat it all. Peyton and I, eyes wide, witness the guys fill their plates, not afraid to reach over everyone to get what they desire.

"Don't be shy," Carson murmurs into my ear, leaning into me.

I meekly spoon spicy crab and brick oven roasted lobster onto the empty square plate in front of me. Carson refills my wine then passes the bottle to Peyton.

"Ladies," Warner calls for our attention, "you'll want to try these oyster shooters and the oysters with Nobu sauce." His wicked smirk dares me to blush.

Always up for anything, Peyton tries each while Warner's eyes are glued to her lips the entire time.

Eli's eyes dart from Warner's to Jake's then mine.

I simply shake my head at their antics; I'm sure an aphrodisiac is the last thing these men need.

When my second glass of wine fades, Carson urges me to drink from my water glass. It's now I realize he isn't drinking alcohol with the rest of us. *Interesting.* The table holds two empty vodka bottles, a wine bottle, and an empty bottle of Jack. Some platters are bare. I easily assess we have more leftovers than what we actually consumed.

The guys are talking more than eating, and with empty beverages, I assume we will leave before reordering. It's a shame so much food will go to waste. What's worse is the price of the uneaten food. I feel guilty. There are many in need, and we squander our meal.

"Have a seat," Warner encourages our waitress as she attempts to exit our private room. His hands pat both his black, jean-clad thighs.

Surprisingly, she sits precariously on one of his knees. He whispers to her softly; as she giggles, her body visibly relaxes.

"Wanna lick?" He pulls his red sucker from his mouth with a pop and taps her bottom lip with it.

She refuses to open or stick out her tongue which causes Warner to laugh deviously.

"Playing hard to get, I see." His hands on either side of her, he lifts her to stand. "Off you go, then." He swats her on the butt.

She emits a squeal as she scurries away.

He turns to Peyton, "You'll have a suck, won't you?" He extends his sucker, and she opens wide for him, her tongue extended. When she closes her mouth, his eyelids grow heavy, and his tongue glides across his lower lip.

"Luke," she says with her mouth full of sucker. "Wanna lick?"

Luke's bright blue eyes react to her flirtation.

My eyes fly to Warner to see his reaction to her sharing his candy. Where I expect to see disgust or betrayal, I find approval. He likes her game. The three definitely imagine something other than a sucker in their mouths and show no shame for speaking loud enough for all of us to hear their foreplay.

9

MONTANA

I marvel at Carson's patience in corralling his band mates from Nobu into the limo. The three are easily distracted by other patrons, hot women, and their cell phones as we exit the restaurant.

Warner informs the group he wants to head to a poker table instead of the night club.

Carson reminds the group, "Meredith scheduled an appearance for us tonight. We can't back out."

"Two hours," Jake pats Warner on the back. "After two hours, we'll head to the casino."

They don't look to Carson for approval.

While the others climb into the limo, Carson turns to me. "Meredith is supposed to be with us for all public appearances. I'm gonna let her have it about ducking out tonight." He shakes his head in frustration then motions for me to climb inside.

Unraveled

Upon exiting the Hummer, a hotel staff member immediately greets us and instructs us to follow her. She leads us through a maze of hallways, out of sight of the other guests. We exit through employee doors and are asked to wait here for a moment. Standing between two large, marble pillars, we're somewhat hidden from others standing in line, surrounded by velvet ropes leading to the doors of the club.

Our guide speaks into her headset, and immediately, a bouncer at the club door looks our way then nods. He speaks to the two security guards commanding the waiting guests.

If Peyton and I were coming to the club, we would be waiting in that extremely long line. As we're hanging with the band tonight, we're escorted past the long line, straight into the club. The club manager and two waitresses greet us and explain where the VIP area is. We follow the scantily clad women.

It amazes me, the speed at which cell phones appear and the number of camera flashes attempting to capture the band walking through the main level of the club. A shiver climbs my spine at the thought that I'll be in the photos, too. I don't know these people; I don't want them to have photos of me.

Carson and the guys smile, wave, and occasionally pose for the crowd as they pass. This is normal for them. I can't imagine living life constantly in the public eye, always available, not able to relax.

Peyton and I attempt to fade into the background, but Carson takes our hands and leads us with the group. Finally, at the stairs to the VIP area, we are no longer visible to the crowd.

We're escorted to a large, oval, high-backed booth facing the floor-to-ceiling glass wall with a view of the club below. Carson motions for Peyton, then Eli, to take a seat. Next, he urges me to slide in before him. Warner, then Jake, scoot in near Peyton.

"Ketel One, Grey Goose, Johnny Black, and …" Warner looks to Peyton for her order.

"Two Stella Artois, please," I order. Turning to the guys, I state, "We're lightweights." I shrug, apologetically.

For once, Peyton doesn't argue with me.

"And, six small bottles of water," Carson adds to the order.

The bottle girl looks back to Warner, bats her fake eyelashes, then wiggles away. I can't help but roll my eyes at the desperation that drips off of her.

"Relax," Carson whispers into my ear.

Goosebumps grow on my skin at this nearness. "So, what exactly happens in the VIP section?" I ask.

"Anything and everything," Warner smirks, eyebrows wagging suggestively.

I quickly move my attention to the dancing crowd below. Like all clubs and bars I've been to, the women outnumber the men, clad in a variety of skimpy dresses, tight pants, and killer heels.

"We can go dance," Carson murmurs.

My head spins to him. *He's kidding, right?* My brow furrows, imagining the chaos of fans, mostly women throwing themselves at him; not to mention the photos.

"Not down there." He motions with his chin to the lower level. "There's a dance floor over there." He points to the right of our booth. Through the glass, I see an open area with VIPs leaning on a railing, looking below.

Before I can tell him I don't want to dance, our waitress returns with our drinks. Carefully, she places the large bottles in the center of the small, round, knee-high table with glasses and tiny water bottles around the edge.

Warner motions for her to come closer by patting his knee. The young woman sits without hesitation. *Is this required in her job description, or does she hope, one day, to be swept away by one of the rich bar patrons?*

"See the girl in the red, sequin dress and her friend?" He points to the dance floor below.

The bottle girl's eyes follow his extended arm and finger before she nods.

"Please invite them to join us." He flashes a devilish grin to the group.

With a nod and an attempt to hide her disappointment, she rises to leave.

Eli stands, stumbling over first mine then Carson's feet in his attempt to catch the waitress. With an arm thrown over her shoulders, he escorts her right up to the glass wall. I can no longer hear the conversation, but as he points below, I assume he's picking out a girl for him, too. As they walk back to our booth, Eli orders six apple martinis and another bottle of vodka.

Sadness washes over me; these men don't lead a normal life. Dating must be difficult, maybe even out of the question. Their version of Tinder is merely pointing and crooking a finger.

Soon, the waitress returns with a tray of drinks and six--yes, six--smiling women following her. Eli welcomes them to join our group as the waitress brings over chairs. I'm not sure how he did it, but Warner has one girl on either side of him in mere seconds. His fingers twist in the curls of one woman as he whispers flirtatiously in the other's ear.

I jump when Carson's heated breath skims my skin.

"Remember when I told you I need my own space to get away?" His lips nearly graze my cheek. My breath catches, and my body heats at his proximity. "It's rarely just the four of us, and I can only endure so much of this." He lifts his chin toward the group.

Before I can reply, a sharply dressed man with what looks like a bouncer, wearing a black t-shirt and black suit approach. He introduces himself as the club owner and thanks the band for coming. A woman approaches, large camera in tow, and directs the men to pose with the owner for some promo photos.

Staring longingly at Warner, one of the new female guests asks the other, "Do you think he wants us both?"

"Does it matter? He's worth millions," the other replies. "Wait until my followers see this on my Insta."

Wow. Just wow. I mean, Peyton likes to get wild and have a good time, but I've never known anyone like these women. A one-night stand, a three-some... They don't care as long as he's rich and famous. I'm sure they don't even know his last name is Bradshaw and chances are, they don't even listen to his music.

The band returns, sliding back into the booth. As Carson and Jake resume their spots by Peyton and me, Warner and Eli each take a girl onto their lap.

I try not to stare, but it's hard. The women all up their game. Their hands often touch or rub legs, chests, and play in hair. After only minutes, Eli stands up with the girl from his lap and leads her, hand in hand, from the room.

Part of me longs to go with him. I'm not sure how much more of the fake giggling I can endure. Warner's friend on his lap rubs against him like a cow at a scratching post.

"Are there clubs like this in Iowa?" Carson asks, turning his back to the three girls Eli abandoned before they can focus their attention on him.

"Um," I grin, "nightlife in Des Moines doesn't even come close. I doubt they even have a VIP section."

Peyton interjects, "They do have a VIP bottle service, but you sit amongst the commoners."

"Do the two of you go to clubs often?" He continues on the topic.

Peyton handles this question. "We go out, just not always to clubs. We call them bars in Iowa, by the way. We enjoy sports bars more than anything."

Warner ignores the squirming play toy on his thighs. "You enjoy sports bras?" he asks Peyton.

She blushes and slowly enunciates, "Sports bars."

"Whew!" Warner rubs fake sweat from his brow. "Sports bras create a mono-boob. Trust me, there's nothing sexy about a mono-boob."

Peyton sips from her water bottle, looking through her eyelashes toward Warner, a smile forming upon her red face.

"And, breasts as glorious as yours must never be a mono-boob." He seems to enjoy the blushing at his topic.

Peyton spews her mouthful of water across the cluttered drink table. "I'm...so...sorry," she sputters.

Warner and Jake delight in her embarrassment. Much to her dismay, Warner dismisses the woman from his lap, positioning himself facing Peyton. Jake's arm slides behind her on the back of the booth. From here, it becomes a game.

Our waitress returns to clear our little table and then a second waitress leaves fresh drinks.

"No more water for you," Warner informs Peyton, licking his lips. He slides a glass of Vodka toward her.

"Find me a bag of Peanut M&Ms," Jake orders the waitress, throwing a one-hundred-dollar bill on the tray she balances in her hand.

With a nod, the bottle girl excuses herself to fill our drink orders and fetch his candy. I find it odd she didn't hesitate or ask any questions at Jake's order. Peanut M&Ms are not a common nightclub snack. Mentally, I map the strip; CVS and Walgreens aren't nearby either.

Carson's hand brushes mine on my lap beside him. "Overwhelming, right?" His lips form a small smile. "I like to believe I'm still normal, but I'm in the band; all of this comes with it."

"I'm sorry if I'm wide-eyed," I tell him honestly, keeping my voice low. "It's a lot to take in. There are so many fans everywhere, eyes are constantly on you, and phone cameras follow you." I shake my head. "Then, there's the women willing to do anything. There's nothing normal about any of it."

"I feel like I don't fit in at these types of events," he confesses.

"I'm not buying that," I challenge. "You definitely belong with a guitar in hand and a mic nearby."

He chuckles, and his smile grows wider. "I feel at home playing music. Performing is in my blood. I'd do it naked without a thought. I lose myself in my guitar and lyrics."

Naked. Did he just say naked? Oh, holy hell. Now, all I can do is see him naked. I imagine corded muscles, taut skin, and ripples down his abdomen. *Hair? Hmm, I wonder if he waxes, shaves, or has chest hair. Or, better yet, a happy trail from his navel leading to his...*

"It's the meet and greets, the appearances like tonight, and the parties that I feel like a fish out of water at. I long to only write and perform." He runs a hand through his soft waves of brown. "It's not possible, so I grin and bear it."

"I mean," he stumbles. "Usually I detest these nights. Tonight, I'm enjoying my time with you and trying to ignore everything else."

As if on cue, Eli saunters back to our group. Warner asks if he lost something. Eli leans towards the guys on the other side of our booth. I can't hear his explanation for returning without the girl, but I can imagine what he says since Warner and Jake reward him with high fives.

10

CARSON

I refuse to high-five Eli's antics. I worry they will cause Montana to believe all of us act like him.

When he plops in the booth next to me, he adjusts himself. "It was an eight on the BJ scale," he loudly announces.

Peyton giggles beneath her hand, her eyes on Montana. Mine are, too, as I attempt to read her reaction. Her lips curl in over her teeth, and her eyes stare at the beer in front of her.

It's hopeless. No amount of apologizing for the band's actions will erase their crazy behavior. I'm living in La La Land if I think she won't be bothered by them and want to spend more time with me.

"I have to admit that's one of the best bathrooms I've ever fooled around in."

I shake my head at Eli's proclamation.

"So," Montana bumps her shoulder against mine. "Have you enjoyed many BJs in public restrooms?"

Jake spits bourbon over his lap and onto the table. Peyton, now sitting on Warner's lap, leans so far back that Jake has to support her head in front of him. "Don't waste alcohol. It's a party foul." She slurs her words a bit. Warner and Eli look to Montana.

"Carson's a party pooper," Eli reports. "He'd rather write or read than get a blow job. You're the first girl he hasn't treated like she has cooties."

"We even started a pool," Warner adds. "We bet on when he'll come out as a gay man."

"He's not gay," Jake's deep voice corrects before he places Peyton back in her upright position.

She spins on Warner's lap, placing her legs over Jake's lap.

"Ignore them," I plead.

"He says that all the time," Warner says. "He acts like it's a sin for us to let loose, have fun, and get our rocks off."

"It's not a sin; it's against the law in public, and it's just not for me," I remind the band while explaining to Montana.

"Hold on, darlin'," Warner tells Peyton as he digs in his front pocket. "Something's popping up."

At his words and devilish smirk, Peyton blushes deep red. This causes Warner's eyes to light up as his smile grows wide.

"Wanna suck?" Warner offers his red sucker. With no answer, he slides the candy along Peyton's lower lip.

I bump my shoulder to Montana's. "Looks like he's set his sights on your friend."

"Should I be worried?" she asks with concern upon her face.

"Peyton seems to give as good as she gets," I quip.

"I'm worried she may have met her match with Warner. She's usually the one in control and making the moves," Montana explains.

"We'll monitor both of them," I promise.

Montana

Though Carson's handsome face and tantalizing conversations entertain me, from time to time, I glance at Peyton. I've noticed she's moved from beer to vodka. Good thing I'm only sipping my beer. One of us needs to make sure we both make it home safely.

She also focuses her attention on both Luke and Warner. I recognize her signature flirty moves. She sets her sights on playing with both men at the same time. I do not understand how she does it.

I watch as a new waitress clears away our empties. Warner murmurs something to her that I don't hear. She leans close and slips a cocktail napkin into his front right jeans pocket, near Peyton's bottom. When she pats the outside of the pocket twice before removing her hand, it's clear she doesn't even try to hide her actions.

Warner smiles at her then leans in to whisper in Peyton's ear. Peyton slaps her palm over her mouth and giggles as she watches the waitress slink away. One hand in Luke's hair, she moves the hand from her mouth and pokes Warner's chest. "You're a bad boy."

Warner grabs her index finger, removes his sucker, and sucks on it.

"Come with me," Carson encourages, taking my hand in his.

I rise, following him from the booth. I nearly walk into the back of him as he suddenly stops at the edge of the booth. When I move my head, peeking around him, I witness a different waitress rub her breasts against Carson's upper arm as she places a white slip of paper in his hand. I'm invisible to her or inconsequential. She giggles, places her hand upon his chest, then pulls away like it's the hardest thing in the world for her to do.

Carson looks to me. "It's best if we just ignore her," he snickers.

I cock my head as my brow furrows.

"I've found if I act like it never happened, they won't approach me again," he explains, embarrassed.

"Luckily for me," Eli murmurs near my ear, standing behind me, his hands on my upper shoulders, "he hands me the info."

I turn my head, looking over my shoulder, my jaw agape as Carson passes the paper to an excited Eli. *Does he have no shame? How many women does Eli need in one night?*

Carson

I release Montana's hand, pulling my cell phone from my pocket. I scroll to Meredith and text her it's time to pick us up. I've had enough for tonight. Although I've enjoyed my conversations with Montana, the antics of my band not only annoy but embarrass me. I'm still unsure if Montana has enjoyed the evening or not.

As much as I want to spend more time with her, I need to write. So many lyrics and chords are swarming my brain. It'll take hours to put them all on paper. Perhaps if she had fun, she'll be up to spending time with me tomorrow.

"I've texted Meredith," I announce to the guys.

"But, Dad, I'm not ready to go home," Eli playfully whines.

"That's between you and Meredith," I retort. "I'm outta here."

I signal a nearby waitress; we are ready for the check.

"I don't think Peyton's ready to return to the hotel, but I am," Montana states beside me.

I attempt to judge her honesty; I catch her in the middle of a yawn, back of her hand over her mouth.

"Not used to the rock star life?" I tease.

"I've been up since eight; can you say the same?" she defends.

"Well..." I hedge, then decide to be honest. "Not exactly. I was up most of the night trying to write, only staring at an empty notebook."

She places her palms upon my chest, looking up at me through her lashes. "Your lyrics speak to the masses. I have faith in you; the words will come."

Her smile, those dimples, her thick lashes—I'd kiss her if I didn't think she'd slap me for being too forward. Dazzled by her looks, I can only nod in reply.

When she pulls her hand from mine, my skin burns. It aches for her return. *How can she affect me so in less than 12 hours?* I join her at the enormous glass wall, the crowd below us moving to the beat, bodies swaying, enjoying each other and the night.

I imagine our bodies close, moving with the beat, hands roaming, in a world where I'm a normal guy, a world where fame isn't an ominous, stone wall between us.

"Yo, Carson," Warner calls over the loud music pumping into the room via the speakers.

Over my shoulder, I spot the club manager and Meredith at the booth. My stomach plummets. My night with Montana is ending. The pull to be near her is as strong as the call to write.

I escort Montana toward the group. Eli rises to stand beside us while Warner, Luke, and Peyton remain seated.

"I'm headed to the poker tables," Warner states firmly, his face close to Meredith's when he stands, wobbles, then rights himself.

"First stop is the hotel," I inform the guys. "The rest is between you and her." I point to Meredith.

I'm ready for them to be her responsibility. I've kept them from scandals and jail so far tonight. It's time for my babysitting shift to end.

Montana

As our entourage reaches the base of the stairs, the crowd turns, phones pop out, and the show begins again. The crowd calls out individual names, hoping a band member will look their way for a photo or autograph.

Hands extend, trying to touch, grab, and stop a celebrity. The guys wave and smile to their fans. Meredith, the club owner, and three beefy bouncers force our group to keep moving toward the door.

I grasp the hem of Carson's shirt with both my hands. It seems the closer we get to the door, the closer the crowd squeezes in. I keep my head down and eyes pinned to his back. I'm aware I'll be in photographs; however, it will only be in profile. The last thing I want is to be in a gossip mag or on social media.

Carson's hand reaches around his back to pull my hand from his shirt and tugs me to his side.

"Just a little further," his low voice promises, tucking me tight to his side.

I guess I wasn't hiding my growing anxiety. I melt into his warmth; he forms a protective cocoon around me.

At the open door, we find sizable crowds on two sides of the red velvet ropes, creating a pathway for us to walk between on our way to safety in the hidden hallways. While the band stops, smiles, and waves, Peyton and I slip safely out of sight.

"Wow," she laughs. "Can you believe we're with the band?"

Enamored by the crowds and the attention they give, she's star struck. I thought fans were always like those at the concerts I've attended; this is different. They seem to disregard all rules and personal space. Tonight, I've witnessed several women making it clear they will do anything with these four famous strangers. The air is heavy with female desperation; I try to shake the fear it brings.

"Carson seems into you," Peyton declares by my side. "He seems like a nice guy, too. Warner and Jake are naughty."

Her smile conveys she likes their kind of naughty. I smile, shaking my head at my best friend. I've never understood how we can be so different yet get along as we do.

Finally, the employee door opens, and loud crowd noises filter in with the guys.

"Is it always this crazy?" I murmur, leaning into Carson as we make our way back through the maze of hallways to the limo.

He shakes his head. "Meredith had an arrangement with the club owner," he explains. "She posted our location on social media. Most of the time, we wait until we've left to post that detail."

"I knew I wasn't the only fan of Communicable. I just never dreamt fans could be this crazy." I fight another yawn.

"Most of that crowd isn't fans of our music." Carson mimics my yawn. "They're attracted to the fame."

I contemplate his words as we slide into the black stretch Hummer outside the hotel. *Would I ever track down someone famous when I read on Instagram that they were nearby? Nope.* I'm a big fan of the band but wouldn't stalk them if I had the chance. Peyton, yes. She'd even drag me along. But I'd hide in the back, at a safe distance. It's what I did when she tried to get us backstage at a concert. I'm good at fading into the background.

Carson taps his index finger between my eyebrows. "What has you concentrating so hard?"

I realize my head is tipped to the side, and my brow is furrowed. "I was just contemplating if I would have hunted the band down when I saw the posts," I confess honestly.

"No," Peyton's voice is much too loud for our enclosed space. "No way. You'd spend the night talking non-stop about Communicable and their music, but you'd stay away."

Everyone's eyes fall on me in the dimly lit interior. I nod then shrug, agreeing with my friend's assessment.

Carson leans closer into me. "Lucky for me you were locked out of your room, then."

All my anxieties from the crowd and cameras fade as I look into his deep, brown eyes and sexy smile. *I'm in so much trouble.*

11

MONTANA

When the limo stops at our hotel, I breathe a sigh of relief; crowds are not waiting for us. One by one, we climb from the back. Eli and Warner require help, having had much more alcohol than the rest of us.

"The poker tables will have to wait until tomorrow." Meredith informs Warner; surprisingly he puts up no fight.

"Party in the penthouse," Eli cheers.

"Count me out," Carson replies. "I will walk Montana and Peyton to their room then write lyrics in my room the rest of the night."

"Actually, if it's alright with you," Peyton places her hands on my shoulders, "I'd like to join them in the penthouse for a while."

Her green eyes search mine while pleading for me to agree. When I nod, she kisses me on the cheek.

"You're the best." Then, she turns to Carson. "You'll see she's safe in the room?"

"Of course," he promises, his hand taking mine.

"Don't do anything I wouldn't do," I warn Peyton.

"Yeah, right," she scoffs.

Carson escorts me through the lobby and casino, towards the bank of elevators.

"She'll be okay?" I ask, concerned for my friend.

"Judging from the attention she received from Jake and Warner, I suspect she'll be just fine. Eli will keep everything under control."

"But he's drunk," I protest.

"He's surprisingly alert, even when his body sways."

I guess I'll trust Carson on this one.

Carson

My mind is a jumble of words that I need to get on paper. It's killed me all night to not even be able to jot them down on a napkin or paper coaster while we were out. I'm headed to my room to write the rest of the night.

"Thank you for an entertaining evening," Montana murmurs as the elevator passes floor after floor. "We got to experience a side of Las Vegas we never thought we would; you guys sure know how to party."

"Correct me if I'm wrong..." I look into her light brown eyes. "Peyton seems to know how to party on her own."

Montana snorts in laughter, covering her face with her hands. Her cheeks pinken with embarrassment.

"We all have our talents," she says. "Yours is writing music and playing guitar; hers is having a good time."

The elevator doors open onto our floor, I motion for her to exit before I follow. I'm torn. In a few, short steps, I'll say good night and head to the solitude of my hotel room. I need to write; I want to write. A large part of me longs to stay with Montana, however; time flies when I'm with her. I'm afraid to say good night as I may never see her again.

"Thanks for everything." Montana's teeth tug at her lower lip. "I had..." she stammers.

"I enjoyed having someone with me," I admit. "It's difficult being

Unraveled

the only sober one, trying to control those three when they drink." I lean my shoulder against the door frame. "What are your plans for tomorrow night?" I hope I'm not being too forward. I don't want to let her disappear; I need to see her again.

"Um..." She shifts her weight from one foot to the other as her right hand plays nervously in her hair. "I must ask Peyton, but I don't think we have any concrete plans."

"Cool," I respond like a goober. "If you give me your number, I can text you in the afternoon to meet for the evening. The guys enjoyed having the two of you with us."

She nods. "Hand me your phone; I'll type it in."

I place my cell in her outstretched hand. She taps a few numbers then passes it back to me. "If you hit send, I'll have you in my contacts, too."

Glancing at my phone, I see she typed her number in the text app. I hit send. Electricity hums in my veins at the knowledge she now has my phone number, too.

"Well," Montana interrupts my thoughts, "I should get inside, so you can..." She motions down the hallway.

"Goodnight." I lean forward, placing a gentle kiss on her cheek. When I pull away, she's stunned. Her eyes scan my face while her index finger connects with her cheek where my lips touched.

I nod towards her hotel door. While she scans her card to enter, I pull away from the door frame where I leaned. "Be sure to use the deadbolt," I remind her. "I'll wait until I hear it."

She flashes me her dimples before slowly closing her door, and I lose sight of her. She turns a lock and slides the deadbolt into place, and I slip down the hall toward my room.

I drop my ink pen, massaging the palm of my right hand with my left. I make a tight fist then release my fingers a few times in an attempt to work out the cramps. I glance at my phone, seeing it shows four a.m. I've been writing for three hours straight. I flip through the pages of my notebook, admiring the full pages of lyrics.

Montana is my cure. Bumping into her in the hallway opened me up. The dam crumbled, allowing my creativity to flow. Page after page, song after song, she's opened my thoughts and feelings up, so I may lay them all out on a page.

Montana

In the room, I sprawl out on my bed. I open my phone, bypass social media, and search for Carson Cavanaugh and Communicable on the internet. I comb through post after post, looking for a reliable source.

In a magazine article, I read that Carson formed his first band in Middle school; Eli, the drummer, was an original member. In high school, they added Jake, the bass player, to the band, and after graduation, Warner, the lead singer, joined them.

He grew up in San Diego where, after high school, Carson stepped from front man to back up vocals and lead guitar. The original band name in middle school was Virus, and it changed in high school to Communicable. The reporter states that Carson writes most of the lyrics for the band; I knew that fact. Following their current world tour, the band plans to head back into the studio to record their third album.

Carson's bandmates refer to him as the father of the group as he tries to keep the guys out of jail, away from bad press, the ER, and even rehab. Carson is quoted as saying, "I like to have fun; I just rarely let go because someone has to monitor the guys."

After the article, I scroll through pictures of the band. Photos of Warner with different women clinging to him fill the screen. It's easy to see that photographers enjoy capturing the lead singer more than the rest of the band.

I'm relieved that I don't gaze at photo after photo of Carson with scantily clad women; I fear I might be jealous. I have no right to feel possessive. We've not even known each other for twenty-four hours, yet I feel so comfortable, like we've been together for a year.

In all my years watching TV and concerts, I never fully understood the lack of anonymity celebs have. Tonight, I witnessed first-hand the constant cell phone cameras pointed at them. There's no privacy. They're constantly asked to give autographs and photos, fans not caring if they interrupt meals or conversations. In public, they're like animals at the zoo.

The women throwing themselves at the guys tonight weren't groupies, more like attention whores. They would do *anything* to hang with someone famous. I scrunch my nose at the next thought to enter my head. *How many STDs and unplanned pregnancies have these four had?*

My finger slides over the mouse pad as I visit fan pages, rock news sites, and the gossip rags. The four appear at openings, release parties, award shows, and clubs together; often, females pose with them. The only constant in all the photos is Carson. With his blank expression, he appears withdrawn. When a woman is beside him, his hand isn't on her; in fact, they don't even touch. The other guys allow the women to drape themselves over them.

I type "Carson Cavanaugh+girlfriend" into my search engine. No results fit my criteria. Surely, he's had a girlfriend. I wonder how difficult it is for the two of them to keep their relationship out of the public eye.

He's much too gorgeous and kind not to have women interested in dating him. I shake away such thoughts. Carson is a rock star, and I'm a twenty-one-year-old trying to decide if I'm going back to college in the fall or finding a job. There's no way that we'll be together in a year. He has his life in Los Angeles after touring with the band while my world is in the center of Iowa.

I clean my face, slip into my pajamas, and rest my head on a pillow. I resign myself to the fact the only place the two of us can be together is in my dreams and happily fall to sleep.

12
CARSON

The Next Morning

I'm on the sofa, watching Eli and Jake argue over the ingredients in an Old Fashioned at the bar in their large suite. We're waiting on Warner to emerge from his room for the day. He kicked two women out an hour ago, so at least we know he's awake.

"You must open that notebook and pick up the pen in order to write lyrics," Eli spouts sarcastically, pointing at the green notebook sitting on the cushion next to me.

I flash him my shit-eating grin then open it, flipping through five pages of new lyrics written last night.

"No way!" Eli sputters. "Atta boy!"

"How?" Jake asks, astonishment upon his face. "What's changed? I mean, don't get me wrong, I'm glad your writer's block lifted."

Eli smirks at me. "She really has an effect on you, doesn't she?"

Jake looks from me to Eli questioningly.

"After meeting her yesterday afternoon, he said lyrics flooded his head," Eli explains.

"Montana?" Jake seeks further clarification.

Eli nods; all eyes focus on me.

"Within 10 minutes of talking to her in the hallway, words came to me for the first time in months." I shrug unable to explain it further.

"Months, you mean years," Eli jeers.

"It's her lips," Warner suggests, dragging into the room. "Her oral skills cured our Carson-boy, didn't they?" He pauses to look at me for a reaction. "I knew she had talents. It's always the sweet, innocent ones that turn into wildcats in the bedroom." Warner laughs with the guys.

"Hey," I bite out. "Be nice. I won't allow you..."

"Easy tiger," Warner raises both palms towards me.

"What's the saying about protesting too much?" Eli teases.

"What are the lyrics to that Beach Boys song? Something about midwest farmers' daughters..." Warner prods further.

"I think he's had enough," Jake tells the group.

"Are we going to sit around here all day? Or do we have plans for tonight?" I ask, ready for a different topic.

"Meredith plans to meet us here at eight," Eli states, sitting beside me and flipping through my notebook.

"Dinner then a club," Warner adds. "We must make an appearance at ten, then we're free the rest of the night."

I don't like those plans, and I can't wait until eight to see Montana. "I think I'll head down to the casino. You can find me at eight." I snag my notebook from Eli and rise from the sofa.

"Will Montana be gambling with you?" Jake asks, surprising me. He's our introvert, happy to lurk in the quiet room until he's forced to see the public.

"I hope so," I answer honestly. "I'm supposed to text her when we know our plans so Peyton and she can join us."

Eli and Jake announce they'll join me in the casino, causing Warner to huff.

"You can't expect me to stay in the suite alone after you kicked out my playthings," he whines. "I guess I can hang with Peyton while you entertain yourselves with Montana."

I watch as Jake's jaw muscle tightens, and his eyes squint at Warner. It seems he likes Peyton; good for him.

"Let's get ready; we'll meet at the casino bar in an hour," I suggest. Not waiting for a response, I exit the suite.

As I walk down the hall, I text Montana our plans for the evening and tell her I'll knock on her door in an hour. She quickly responds with a thumbs up emoji.

I'm five minutes early when I rap on her door. I'm anxious to see if she's ready. I imagine we'll have to wait on Peyton.

"Come in," Peyton invites, holding a tissue in my face. "You'll need this."

I take the proffered tissue, and confused by her words, I raise my eyebrow.

"It's for the drool. Trust me," she promises.

Montana emerges from the restroom, causing my eyes to bulge and jaw to drop.

"I told you." Peyton nudges my shoulder. "She looks hot as hell."

I try to collect myself. I know Montana affects me. Yesterday, in the hallway, she quickly worked me up. I found her adorable and cute; it was her personality that pulled me to her. I shouldn't be surprised that when she dresses up to go out on the town, she's a knockout.

My eyes take her in from top to toe. Her hair is up with curls in the back and two tendrils down to frame her face. Her eyes pop with smoky colors on her lids and black eye liner edging them. Her pink-gloss lips from yesterday are now red with lipstick, luring me to lick and suck upon them.

Her long, bare neck begs to be nipped. Her black halter dress exposes her bare shoulders that invite me to touch and hints to cleavage that I long to lick. *Heaven help me. How will I keep my hands to myself all night?* I'm being tested, and I fear I'm failing miserably.

"Well?" Peyton nudges me again.

I shake away my inappropriate thoughts, scrambling to collect my wits.

"Um," I struggle to find words to express how she looks.

"I told you." Peyton hugs Montana. "He's speechless."

"Ladies," my voice shakes, so I clear my throat. "You look amazing. I'm going to spend the entire night keeping the guys away from you."

"No need." Peyton swats at me. "I can handle myself." She smiles proudly.

I take Montana's hand in mine, pulling her towards me. When she's mere inches from me, I murmur, "You look amazing."

Her brown eyes look up through her velvety-black lashes. Her eyes sparkle, and her skin glows. I want to push Peyton out the door, lock the weird-looking deadbolt, and ravish Montana all night long.

"This will be a very long night," I groan near her ear. I catch a whiff of her light, vanilla perfume. As if she needed help being edible.

Montana

I stifle my giggle at Carson's reaction, while inside, I love that I affect him so. Peyton and I decided to dress up this evening as it's our last in Vegas. We wear our little black dresses and new shoes we purchased in the hotel shops. Although I protested, Peyton styled my hair and applied my makeup; she's much better at it than I am.

I stare up at Carson nervously, and his warm breath caresses my cheeks with his every exhale. In a moment of strength, I place my palms flat upon his chest, rise on my tiptoes, and whisper into his ear, "Should I go change?"

I pat his shoulder as I pass by him to the bedside table to fetch my clutch. Aware that his eyes follow me, I put a little more sway in my hips. I peek inside my bag to ensure I have cash, my debit card, and my ID. When I glance in his direction, he's staring at me.

13

MONTANA

Peyton enters the elevator first, presses the button for the casino, then leans against the rail on the left side of the car. Carson's hand never moves from the exposed skin at the small of my back where the warmth from his hand heats my entire body.

Man buns were never my thing. However, Carson sports one today, and I'm loving it. *Holy hotness. Who knew he could look even better than yesterday?*

His dark dress pants cling tight to his thighs and glutes. His button-down, royal-blue dress shirt accentuates his athletic build. His biceps bulge against the silky fabric. My breath catches at the thought of the silky fabric brushing against my bare skin.

"Everything okay?" Carson asks.

As we plummet, I cover my mouth to hide my giggle. In the metal reflection on the opposite wall, I see Carson raise an eyebrow and erupt with giggles.

"She's always uncomfortable in quiet elevators," Peyton tells him. "Something about needing to break the silence, even with strangers."

Carson's hand slips from my back to my hip, spinning me to face him. "What shall we talk about?"

I stand, frozen in his gaze. I focus on his hair, his man-bun. His wavy, brown hair with perfectly placed highlights calls for my fingers to tangle in it. The scruff dusting his jawline draws my eyes to his mouth and plump lower lip. Oh, those lips; I long to suck his lower one into my mouth and nip it playfully. I startle as the doors open, and the loud casino noise surrounds us.

"Nice chat," Carson teases, motioning us from the car.

Carson

I let the ladies exit before me as I stay near Montana. My hand returns to her back; this dress pushes all of my buttons. With so much bare skin on display, I long to strip it off of her and reveal the rest of her.

"Where are we meeting?" Peyton inquires over her shoulder.

"The casino bar in the center," I share. "What can I get you to drink?"

Peyton orders an apple-tini, and Montana requests a Captain Morgan and diet cola. I flash a glare at a guy I catch staring at Montana from across the bar.

"Fuck," Warner greets. "Those dresses are the shit." His eyes scan Peyton from head to toe and back up.

Eli appears at Montana's side, turning to face her he states, "Carson's gonna have his hands full, keeping guys off of you tonight."

Montana

"Stop," I beg. "It's just a dress."

"Uh-huh," he laughs. "And, the Great Wall of China is just a fence."

I swat him playfully. I love him, because he's different, bright, nerdy, and so much fun to be around. How he comes up with all of his sayings baffles me. "The Great Wall of China a fence!" I love it.

"I'm headed to poker," Warner announces.

Jake nods, and Peyton follows them toward the high stakes area.

"What should we do?" Eli asks.

"I like video slots," I remind them.

"Let's make a lap until a machine calls to us," Eli suggests.

"I like the James Bond, Britney Spears, and Monopoly games," I inform him as we walk. "Oh, and I won on the Buffalo game yesterday."

"Then, let's go find them," Carson agrees.

"Hold on," I order, pulling my cell from my clutch. I open my Casino app, select NYNY, type in James Bond, and the map shows me where to find the game. "It's this way."

"How'd you do that?" Carson asks.

"It's an app. You can find a map of each hotel and casino floor, your favorite games in each, and it even helps you locate your friends."

He hands me his cell. "Download it for me, please."

I take his cell to download the app as I move us toward the machine I want to play. I pass the phone back as we approach and find the 007 game empty, so I quickly take a seat.

"Ah, ah, ah..." I place my hand over the slot when Carson attempts to slide his one-hundred-dollar bill inside for me. "If it's not my money then it's not my luck."

Without argument, he allows me to remove money from my clutch and insert it into the machine. I choose max bet, the machine springs to life. The bonus game hits, I spend the next few minutes choosing cards, matching Bond characters, and piling up more winnings. Over and over, I pick and match cards. My heartbeat races faster as the money grows. $100, $200, $300 and still rising. I match a few more cards and characters. $400, $500, $600... That's when the coin bonus spins begin. When all the games and free spins end, my first spin on this machine rewards me with $1,592 and some odd change. Eli and Carson cheer loudly behind me while I sit, stunned.

Eli orders drinks from a passing waitress while we wait for the casino personnel to fill out the paperwork, gather my information, then fetch me my check and tax form.

"Here I thought you were the lucky one." Eli swings an arm over Carson's shoulders. "Your writer's block lifted when you met her, but she's the lucky one. Two big wins in two days—girl, you are the shit."

"I am lucky," Carson states. "Luckily, I went to my room at the right time to bump into Montana." His eyes bore into mine. "The luckiest man alive."

Carson

We sit at the casino bar after Eli and I lose a couple hundred each on machines. Montana carries all the luck in our trio.

She slowly sips her Captain and diet while Eli and I enjoy beers. When she finishes her third drink, she states she'll have no more until she eats.

"Where are we eating?" I ask, turning to Eli.

He beams. "It's my night to choose, so it'll be Twin Peaks."

I can't even act surprised; it's so totally Eli. Burgers, fries, beers, and boobs in a super casual setting. I can't help the enormous smile upon my face. Meredith joins us tonight, and watching her endure Twin Peaks will provide hours of entertainment for the four of us. Tonight's looking better than last night already.

"I'm sending a group text to meet in the lobby in fifteen minutes," I tell them as my fingers work on my phone screen.

When I look up, I spy two guys across the bar, staring at Montana. I fight a growl as I slip from my stool. "Let's make our way to the lobby," I suggest, not letting on that I'm attempting to sneak her away from all lecherous eyes. As hot as I find her bare skin in the dress, I'll have to fight off men all night.

Montana

"Where are we eating?" Peyton asks, louder than she should.

"Well," Eli moves closer, "I'm glad you asked. Tonight, we'll dine on the best American cuisine accompanied by the coldest beer served in frosty mugs."

Peyton raises an eyebrow.

"Twin Peaks," Jake informs, his eyes searching my face for a reaction.

"I love that place!" Peyton cheers. "We have one in Des Moines. They have great appetizers."

I find Carson's eyes still on me. I smile, letting him know I'm not offended by the busty theme of the restaurant.

Meredith doesn't join us at the table, although there's an empty chair. Instead, she stands at the bar, her attention on her cell phone.

Warner instructs the server to bring a round of tequila shots for the group. She turns on her fuzzy-lined hiking boots, shaking her ass on her way to the bar.

"Which app is your favorite?" Jake asks Peyton.

She shrugs, glancing at the menu Warner holds out on her other side. "I like them all."

"Then, it's settled," Warner smiles, wrapping his arm behind her on the chair. He signals the server over again. "We'll take one of each appetizer."

Too much food, especially French fries, and three giant, frosty mugs of beer later, I excuse myself to the ladies' room, and Peyton joins me. I pause at the entrance, staring at the signs on the two doors.

"Which one is the women's?" Peyton asks, confused like me.

I attempt to focus my beer-logged brain. Both wooden signs have a stick figure followed by a "2" and a "P". I point as I speak, "2P means 'to pee'. That one 'stand to pee', this one 'sit to pee'."

"Holy crap." Peyton pushes the 'sit to pee,' door open. "They should warn you about these signs before they serve you three beers."

"Right?" I agree, giggling and following her inside.

The rest of the night passes too fast. With Meredith accompanying us, Carson and I take part in several rounds of shots. The band is recognized the moment we enter the club. Everywhere we look, we're captured on cell phones. I've now learned the VIP area is safer as the cameras can't record everything we do. We're on the second floor; guests downstairs only see us when we lean on the railing, open to the dance floor below. A new, up-and-coming alt-rock band sits near our table. They don't approach but nod, smiling to greet the guys.

Like last night, bottles and drinks rarely remain empty for a minute before the servers swoop in with fresh ones. Life seems easy in VIP-land.

14

MONTANA

The Next Morning

"Make it stop," I groan, placing a pillow over my face to block out the much-too-bright sun as the incessant pounding continues. "Uh," I whimper, clutching the pillow tight at my ears. I've never had a hangover that caused such a loud pounding in my head.

"Montana," a woman yells. "Open your door." Immediately, the annoying pounding resumes.

I throw the pillow from my face, moaning as I roll to place my feet on the floor of the spinning room.

"Hey, why'd you do that?" Carson grumbles from the other side of my bed. I freeze, staring dumbfounded.

Well, I guess that happened. I search my foggy brain; I can't recall the two of us returning to my room.

"Montana," the woman's voice calls again from the other side of the door.

I grab a t-shirt from the floor, pulling it over my head while approaching the door. I quickly check to ensure it's long enough to cover my naked parts. When I turn the handle, the door flies open.

"He's over there," I mumble. Carson's band manager barges past me into my room as I walk into the bathroom and close the door behind me.

I scoop cold water from the faucet to my mouth, hoping to remove the dry, cotton sensation. The cold water brings the urge to potty. I pee and pee and pee. I turn on the water and quickly wash my hands, wanting to return to Carson to seek information about last night.

"Ouch!" I look from the mirror to see what scraped the palm on my right hand. It's a large ring. Not just *any* ring. A giant diamond on my ring finger. I squint at it, the water still flowing from the faucet; I stare as if the diamond will tell me all that I can't remember.

Carson

The faint sound of a phone ringing slices into my sleep. *Is it the room phone?* While my groggy brain dashes between sleep and waking up, the sound of the ringing phone ceases. Replacing it is the sound of heavy pounding on the door.

"Carson, I know you're in there! Open the goddamn door!" Meredith, our band manager yells in her annoying, nasally voice. "Montana," she yells. "Open your door." Immediately, the annoying pounding resumes.

Suddenly, a pillow lands upon my face.

"Hey, why'd you do that?" I grumble from my side of the bed.

I toss the pillow back to Montana's side. While I attempt to keep my eyes open, I adjust myself under the sheet, and I wonder which one of the guys stirred up trouble, causing Meredith's tirade so early in the morning. I also wonder how she knew to look for me in Montana's hotel room.

Propping myself up on another pillow, I squint, unable to focus on Meredith storming into the room, coming to stop at the foot of the bed.

How is it this woman looks perfectly put together in her black pencil skirt, blue silk blouse, and matching high heels? It's much too early. Her hands planted on her hips and her blue, open-toed shoe tapping, she glares at me as though it's my turn to talk.

"Where is your cell phone?" she huffs.

I couldn't begin to guess where, in this room of empty bottles and clothes strewn on the floor, to find my phone.

"Clearly you haven't been on social media today?" When I don't respond, Meredith continues, "You two have created a cluster fuck. What were you thinking?"

"What's up?" I ask my manager.

"What's up?" she spits back, her voice raised. "What's up? I'll tell you what's up… "

"We've got a problem," Montana blurts, returning from the bathroom, her hands tangled in her messy hair.

"I'm glad to see one of you is thinking clearly this morning," Meredith spouts.

I look from her back to Montana whose long, shapely legs disappear under a large black t-shirt announcing, "I'm the Groom." I'd chuckle at it if my head didn't hurt. With effort, I lift my eyes toward her face. The fingers of her left hand wave in the air. It's there that I see she's wearing a ring. *Fuck! Did I sleep with a married woman?*

"Yes, you idiot," Meredith hisses. "She's your wife."

Wife? Did she say my wife? Fuck! I pull my left hand off my morning wood to find a gold band wrapped around the base of my ring finger.

"How'd you let this happen?" I ask my manager.

"Me? I didn't let this happen. Your group snuck off while I was loading Warner's drunk ass in the limo," she defends. "I can't be in charge of the four of you all the time. Of all the band, you're the last one I'd worry about fucking up this majorly."

"The internet is crawling with photos and videos of the two of you last night," she adds. "Seems you didn't rush back to the room to start the honeymoon." She sighs heavily. "That would have been *too* easy."

Montana and I scramble to find our phones. She finds a video first. "My family's gonna kill me," she whispers. When she turns the volume on, I hear, "Meet my husband, Mr. Cavanaugh," in Montana's voice. "Meet my wife, Mrs. Cavanaugh," in my voice. Then, "Can we take a selfie with the happy couple?" in an unknown, male voice.

"Meredith," I raise my voice to get her attention, "Montana and I need some time. Can I text you later?"

Hands on her hips, Meredith states, "Flight is at two, so don't take too long." She gives Montana a disapproving snarl before leaving the room.

At the sound of the door latching, I ask, "Can we talk?"

"My parents are gonna kill me," Montana murmurs, barely above a whisper.

"Please shut your phone off, so we can avoid social media. The vultures are swarming, and they show no mercy. They're mean, evil really, with their comments. They're out to entertain their followers and viewers, not caring if it's truthful or who it hurts. Trust me, I've been through it many times with the guys in the band. However, this is the first time I'm the subject," I ramble. "Where is it? I'll turn it off for you."

"I should at least text my parents to let them know I'm okay," Montana protests.

"Let me open the phone, type the text, and send it for you. That way I can protect you from missed calls, texts, and social media alerts a bit longer," I offer.

After I send the text for her, Montana rests her forehead to the wall of windows, eyes staring down the Strip.

"I need to look up a few things; it will just take a minute," I tell her back. "Then, we'll work this all out."

Palms pressed to the cold tile, I allow the hot water from the shower head to soak my hair and pelt my body.

Where did I go wrong? When did I cross the line? I drank way too much. Oh, what she must think of me... I never let my guard down like last night. It's like I did everything I harp on the guys not to do. Three condoms. There are three used condoms in the trash by the bed. Why can't I remember the sex? Three condoms mean it should be memorable.

We are good together. Two days felt like years, so natural. Then, I self-sabotaged by marrying her. The paparazzi will love a chance to spoil my clean, rocker boy image. I'm far from perfect, definitely no choir boy. They'll have a field day with this.

No way she'll want to keep in touch after the annulment. It will end our good thing. Is there any way possible, even drunk, she meant her vows at the ceremony?

I've gotta find a way not to lose her; it's clear I need her in my life. Within an hour of meeting her and chatting, lyrics swam in my head as never before. She's more than a muse; sitting by her, my soul found its match, and I felt complete for the first time. Without touching or kissing, I knew we'd make a great pair. It just felt right, similar to my moving to lead guitar and bringing Warner in on lead vocals. It's meant to be. But there's no way Meredith will let me keep her.

I like her; I like her a lot. I've never felt this way, this close with another woman, even after several dates. She's one of a kind; she's my kind. I need her on a visceral level. She breathes life into my creativity while she ignites a yearning within me.

Even now, lyrics come to me. *I need to write; I must record them.* She gifts me word after word, verse after verse.

I emerge from the hot shower, soaking wet with a towel around my waist, leaving a water trail from shower to sink. I frantically search the restroom, looking for my notebook. Not seeing it, I scramble for any paper and pen or other writing utensil.

Not finding anything better, I use a black eyeliner pencil on the enormous mirror over the vanity.

I must ask Montana if she has any paper I may use to copy these lyrics onto.

Unraveled

With a towel around my waist, I rub a hand towel through my wet hair, stepping from the bathroom.

Montana stands at the large windows, her forehead pressed to the glass and the desert sun's rays enveloping her. She's still wearing the "I'm the Groom" shirt, her legs, golden tan, spilling from its back hem mid-thigh. I need my cell phone; I want a photo to remind me of this moment forever. Unaware I'm watching her across the room, she presses her arms to the window over her head. I stifle the moan in my chest as the hem rises several inches, revealing a peek of the lower portion of her bare ass. As if her tone legs didn't do it for me, her exquisite backside assures me every inch of her is magnificent.

I don't recall last night, and my hands itch to explore her as if for the first time, my mouth to taste her, and my body to please her. She's definitely a temptation I can't let escape. I dress quickly in my jeans from last night, skipping my day-old boxers. Then, I purposely bump the bathroom door, the noise a signal I'm behind her.

She turns from her contemplation above the Strip and curls a knee beside her on the bed. *This woman is killing me with her no underwear poses. I must think of something else, anything else.*

"Do you have any paper I could use?" I ask, slicing into the much too quiet room.

She pulls a journal from her luggage. She opens to the first clear page and passes it to me, eyes questioning.

"Some lyrics came to me in the shower; I wrote them on the mirror and need to copy them, so I don't lose them."

"May I see?" She whispers.

I'm sure she's worried I won't share my work until it's perfect. That's not me. I crave input and reaction. I want to see how my words affect her and ask what she thinks of them.

When I nod, she follows me. "I need to buy you a new eyeliner pencil," I mention as she enters the bathroom.

I watch her almond-shaped, brown eyes grow wide, her head tilt to the side, and her lips part. I swear I hear her whisper, "Oh."

I follow her eyes as they read down the mirror, then start over at the top. This time she speaks the words, barely a whisper. When she's done, she looks to me, and I find tears in her eyes; she's trying hard to keep them from falling. My chest swells and warmth fills my body that my words move her so.

Montana

I lean my forehead against the cool window glass. Though my eyes peer toward the Vegas Strip, I see nothing. The cool air-conditioner feels good upon my face. *I'm married. I got drunk and married to a guy I met only two days ago. I married a freaking rock star.*

My parents will be ashamed; they raised me better than this. They instilled in me that marriage isn't a frivolous endeavor and should be a lifelong promise.

My older brother will kill me. I fear his impending lecture more than my father's. An annulment is a quick fix for a fuckup. Carson's too good to be a fuckup. He's so sweet.

When he sat by me in the hallway, a cozy, warm feeling enveloped me. Not a liquid sensation, a full, complete feeling. I'm me with him. I'm not fake. Carson is a gentleman. I haven't had a first date since high school that the guy didn't try for more at least once. Two days together, dates of sorts, and he only kissed me once. Well, once that I remember, then we got married.

Talking to him is as easy as talking to Peyton. It's as if he's familiar, not a total stranger. Carson loves his friends despite their flaws and helps look out for them. He's hot as hell—that shouldn't matter—it's a nice perk.

A pit grows in my stomach at the thought of getting an annulment and never seeing him again. I feel that if we get an annulment, it will be my biggest mistake in the eyes of my parents with the wedding a close second.

Could it work?
Could we try?
Should we try?
Do I want to try?
Would he?

"Okay," Carson clears his throat, pulling me from my thoughts; I turn from the windows to face him. He pats the bed beside him in invitation.

I comply, leaning against the headboard with a pillow hugged tight to my chest.

Beside him on the bed, I can feel his heat, even with our bodies not touching. Neither of us speak, lost in our own thoughts.

"This may sound crazy, but hear me out," he begins, voice tight. "What if we stay married?"

Stay married. Did he just suggest we stay married? I expected he'd lobby for a quickie annulment and hop on his jet, never to see me again.

"You see," he stumbles a bit as his voice falters, "I like you. A lot. I mean..." He runs both hands through his damp hair. "What I'm proposing is not to get the annulment, then go our separate ways. Instead, we continue to learn more about each other. Kind of like we're dating. There's no rush, because we can get a divorce anytime. But..."

I toss the pillow aside, turn to face him, eager to hear more.

"It feels real to me. There's something about you. I feel... Every part of me... I think I'd never forgive myself if I didn't give this a try. I mean..." he turns his body to face me. "I mean everything up to the drunken wedding was pretty amazing."

Carson

"Right," she nods. "I know an annulment will upset my family even more than learning we married."

"Mine will see it as an escape clause," I admit.

"Ya, a quick fix to easily erase it." Her eyes seem to search me. "Do you think we..." she motions between us with her index finger. "Could we make us work?"

"I think so." *Oh, how I hope so. I believe she's what's been missing in my life.*

"Me, too," she agrees.

"An annulment now or a divorce three months from now... Either way, my parents will be just as disappointed." I share.

"Maybe if they see us try to take the marriage seriously, they'll back off a little," she offers, a smile slipping onto her lips. A little light sparkles in her eyes. "I didn't want to do the annulment and never see you again."

"Me either; that was all I could mull over in the shower. Two nights isn't enough. You leave me wanting more, so much more." I confess. "You're easy."

She raises a single eyebrow.

Montana

"I didn't word that right." He immediately raises his hands, crossing them as they wave between us.

"And you call yourself a songwriter, a master of words, if you will," I tease.

"Well, until we met in the hall, words evaded me for over a year," He states, baring his truth to me.

"Wait." I quickly stand. "You mentioned that last night. I remember we were in a taxi; the four of us snuck out when Meredith loaded the guys into the limo."

I anxiously wait to hear if he remembers more.

"Remember? We were going shopping," I nod, attempting to coax his memory.

He shakes his head. Maybe memories will come back later today. "Are we really gonna do this?" He seeks assurance.

"I want to," I say. "But what happens next? We're scheduled to fly in opposite directions this afternoon."

His eyes plead with mine. His eyebrows are high, eager for my answer.

I open my mouth, but no words escape. I raise my hand to my lips as I search for the strength to tell him how I feel; I nod.

Unraveled

Carson

I'd give anything to see her smiling dimples rather than the sadness and pain she expresses now. "My parents won't like my disregard for the sanctity of marriage," I share, matching her thoughts with total honesty.

"My parents constantly lecture my brother and me that marriage is forever, requires work, and requires patience to be successful," she states, eyes downward. Looking up through her long lashes, she quirks her mouth to one side and shrugs.

"Exactly," I agree. "I even promised my family I'd never treat relationships like rock stars usually do," I sigh. "And, look what I did; we're all over the internet." I stand, walking to the foot of the bed to grab my phone. "I've worked hard to portray a clean rocker image, and a drunken Las Vegas wedding followed by a quick annulment will tarnish that image. The paparazzi have tried for years to catch me in a situation every other rocker appears in regularly."

"I get it," she states. "I've strived to uphold the values my family holds dear. Our marriage will not please them, and I don't want to disappoint them."

"So, you'd be willing to stay married?" I ask.

She nods slowly.

"I have an idea about how we can move forward." I return to sit beside her, back against the headboard. "We're scheduled to record our next album in L.A. next week. We stay in a house together and use its studio. The label arranges it all." I shake my head slightly, running my hands over my stubbled jaw. "We've done this for past albums, and because it's L.A., Warner will sneak out to party, only to show up hungover in the studio the next day. Eli will parade girls through every night then be too exhausted to contribute during our studio session. Jake... Well, Jake is a mystery; I have no idea where he traipses off to." I take her hand in mine. "We're supposed to work morning, noon, and night. The goal is to release our best work in the least amount of time."

My thumb rubs absent-mindedly on the back of her hand.

Montana

I do my best to concentrate on his words as he shares his idea with me, but I fail. My body's reaction to his gentle touch grows exponentially. My mind drifts to him caressing other parts of my body, causing me to miss his entire plan.

"So," Carson drawls out, "what do you think?" His eyes ping pong back and forth, searching mine.

I blow out a long breath as I search my brain for any clues to the plan he shared; I've got nothing. "Sounds good to me," I lie. *Well, is it a lie if I don't know what I'm agreeing to?*

"Awesome!" Carson taps on his phone several times, then his thumbs type. "I'm scheduling a band meeting in my room in 15 minutes. I need to apologize to the band for the negative publicity. We'll share the plan with them and see if they'll agree."

Carson

Of course, Meredith shows up early for the meeting. I don't want to deal with her crap, but I know it's best to get it over with sooner rather than later.

When I open the door, Meredith plows inside. "I want to handle this before the label calls me in hopes of appeasing them. And, they could call any minute. I've got the paperwork for the two of you to read, and I have a lawyer on standby. When I text, he'll come witness the signatures and file your annulment paperwork."

"Hold your horses," I tell her. "Montana and I talked. We're married; it's a done deal, so move on."

Meredith looks at the two of us, "But…"

"No!" I raise my voice. "There's nothing to say, nothing to argue about. We're adults, and we've come to an agreement to make the marriage work."

Her mouth opens and closes like a fish out of water. She fans herself with an envelope in her hand while she paces from the windows to the door and back. It dawns on her what she's waving.

"Here," she passes the large brown envelope to me. "If you plan to remain married, you need to see this."

"What is it?" I ask, not opening the clasp to peer inside.

"I had a technician run a background check on her for you," Meredith confesses proudly.

"And, what did you find?" Montana coaxes.

Meredith's eyes look from me to her. "I haven't had time to look through the information; I only just received it."

"Let me save you the time." Montana takes the envelope from me and tosses it toward Meredith's chest. "I was born and live in Des Moines, Iowa. My father owns a large farm north of the city, and my mother runs her family's real estate business. They own several properties throughout the metro. I graduated from Lincoln High School and just graduated from Des Moines Area Community College, both with a 4.0 average."

Montana looks to me, her back toward Meredith. "I have no college debt, no credit card debt, and I own my vehicle. I'm not behind on any bills, I live at home, and I've never looked into my credit rating as my parents still pay for everything. But I imagine, should one care to look into it, my credit rating is impressive."

I smile, shaking my head at her. She's sharing information to help us as a newly married couple, but she's also putting Meredith in her place. She licks her lips, smirks, then winks at me before turning to face Meredith, nearly toe to toe.

"Did I forget to share anything?" Montana taunts. "Ask me."

Meredith leans around Montana to look in my direction. "You'll have your hands full with this one."

I'm not sure how to take that from her. For one, Meredith is a type A personality, works twenty-four seven, and wins most of her pissing matches. *Does she mean it as a compliment that she sees Montana as an equal? Or, does she mean Montana's behavior is out of line, and she will cause trouble for me and my band?*

I take the envelope from Meredith, tear it into four pieces, then toss it into the trash can by the desk. I breathe a sigh as there's a knock at my door.

Montana

A knock at the door startles me; one arm remains wrapped across my stomach as my other hand flies to my mouth. Carson smiles sweetly in my direction as he prepares to open his hotel room door.

"Atta boy," Eli greets, pulling Carson in for a one-armed man hug with heavy pats to his back. "I can tell by the looks of the two of you that your wedding night rocked."

Peyton pushes her way past the guys, making a beeline for me. "Oh. My. God. Why didn't you text me back this morning?" She wraps me tight in her embrace, rocking us back and forth.

"Carson shut my phone off until the dust settles." My small voice keeps my words between the two of us.

"Well, your mom lit my phone up, because you wouldn't answer."

Peyton's hands upon my shoulders keep me in front of her; I can't hide my reactions from her eagle-eye gaze.

"I'm still in shock," I confess. "Waking up married... I mean... How do I deal with that?"

She cocks her head to the side, pursing her lips, and blinking several times.

"Hey Meredith," Warner's loud voice draws our attention. "Choir boy's impromptu wedding tops anything I've ever done, right?"

Meredith shakes her head.

"Take a seat," Carson orders, organizing the entire group.

"Dude, we should move up to the penthouse, so there's room to sit," Eli grumbles.

"Sit," Carson demands, pointing to the king-sized bed.

Taking Carson's hand, I'm pulled to his side.

"Ah... They're still wearing the shirts we bought them," Eli points out, looking to Peyton.

So caught up in our situation, I need to look to see what shirts we're wearing. Carson has on the "I'm the groom" t-shirt I threw on when Meredith woke us up. I have on a matching "I'm the bride" t-shirt.

"You bought these?" I look at my best friend.

"Duh," Peyton replies, squinting her eyes.

"So," Carson interrupts, pulling attention back to him, "by now, you know Montana and I were drunk and apparently got married last night."

"Hold on," Eli butts in. "You're playing this off as a drunken mistake?"

Peyton scoffs, walking toward me. "Don't do this," she pleads. "Don't blame it on too much alcohol. It was a great night."

"Was it?" I ask, needing details.

Her eyes squint, assessing.

"Imagine Meredith banging on my door, waking us up, and finding ourselves married."

Eli stands now. "You don't remember?" he asks me, concern painted on his pinched brows.

I shake my head.

"Peyton and I would not have allowed the two of you to go through with it if we thought you were that drunk."

Peyton chimes in, "You seemed very aware of the whole thing. I mean, you came up with your own vows and everything."

I look to Carson to see if he remembers our vows; he's as lost as I am.

Carson speaks to Peyton and Eli. "Please take a seat, so we can continue with the meeting."

Carson

I scan my band members. "First, I want to apologize for the publicity storm you woke to this morning. I'm sorry my actions last night might have placed you in a negative light because of your association with me."

Lying starfish-style on my bed, Eli raises his head. "Negative, dude. Your marrying Montana did not put a blemish on Communicable." He scoffs. "There's a bit of speculation, but your 'Prince of Rock' image remains untarnished. Fans want to know all about the girl that stole your heart."

"Well, trust me when I say, my actions last night were careless on my part. I would have liked to drink less and remember every second of it."

Laughter fills the room.

"You don't..." Jake laughs.

"Neither of us remembers much from the time we left the club," Montana confesses.

"Seriously?" Peyton asks, voice rising as she moves to stand beside her friend. "You didn't seem wasted. Did she?" She looks to Eli for confirmation. Turning back to Montana, she states, "You have to know I'd never let you do such a thing if I thought you were drunk."

Montana takes Peyton's hand, nodding.

"Before we get into the details of last night, I'd like to share an idea with the band and put it to a vote," I interrupt the murmurs throughout the room.

With no objections, I continue. "Montana and I decided to give this marriage thing a go. We're going to spend some time together and see if it's possible for us to remain husband and wife. We've opted not to get the annulment Meredith arranged." I look from Eli to Jake to Warner.

"To allow us more time together, I reached out to Corey. He graciously offered for us to record in his lake home near Des Moines this summer. Montana and I will head to L.A. I'll pack, then we will fly to Des Moines to arrange everything at the house before you arrive. Corey assures me everything we need is in the studio, and he has a local guy that will assist us with recording any time we'd like."

I scan the room again to find no argument and no questions from the band.

"Carson, no!" Meredith interjects, authoritatively.

Montana

"Meredith, this is not up for debate. Montana and I plan to take some time, learn more about each other, and not get an annulment. We've enjoyed the past two days and don't want to throw that away." He squeezes my hand as his eyes meet mine for a moment.

Meredith points her glare in my direction. Her tight lips and squinted eyes attempt to intimidate me.

"An annulment is the best way to put an end to this social media nightmare," she hisses. "We'll play it off as publicity for the new album. I'll release a statement that it was research for lyrics you're working on."

Hands on hips, left foot pointed outwards, she stands firm in front of Carson and me.

"Hear me. Listen to me this time," Carson snarls. "There will be no annulment. No. Annulment."

He leans closer to her, still holding my hand. "You work for us, not the other way around. If you have a problem with the band's plans, you're welcome to request the label reassign you. Now, step back so I can talk to the band."

Meredith steps back, her icy glare stopping on me as she walks by.

Carson draws in an audible, calming breath, squeezing my hand then relaxing his grip. He licks his lips, nods, then returns to the previous conversation.

"Here's where I'd like to propose something, and then, we'll vote on it." He waits for each of the guys to nod before continuing. "I've contacted Corey to take him up on his offer to record in his studio. ZipTie's in the middle of their world tour, so he said we can use his lake house and studio for the summer."

The guys shuffle a bit in their positions. I can tell they are hesitant about this change in plans. I listen intently as I didn't hear him when he shared the plan with me earlier.

"We can't change plans one week before recording," Meredith states.

Carson holds his palm out in her direction. "I've already contacted the label, and since Corey's not charging us, they'll save money."

Meredith scoffs. "There's no way Corey's footing the bill all summer. And, we still need to discuss the annulment."

"We won't pay for the house or the studio time," he shoots a glare at Meredith. "The label will cover food, utilities, and staff during our stay. As the label comes out ahead, they are on board with the change of location."

Meredith, shocked at his thoroughness, is silent.

"By leaving L.A., we'll focus on the album more and will finish it faster. Of course, Montana's from Des Moines, so by recording at Corey's, we'll be able to see each other and give this relationship a try."

"I'm in," Eli blurts. "I've never been to Iowa."

Jake grunts, "I'll go if everyone wants to."

All eyes swivel to Warner who rolls his eyes. "You seriously expect us to give up L.A., fly to Iowa, and rough it for the summer?"

I'm astonished the guys don't correct his statement; instead, they remain quiet.

"I will not leave the ladies behind in L.A. to hook up with the cows in Iowa," Warner whines.

It takes all of my willpower not to bite back at his dis of my home state. He essentially called Peyton and I cows, inferior to the women in L.A. I admit I'm not a fake blonde with fake hair extensions and fake body parts; I may not look as hot as the ladies he sleeps with then tosses to the side, but I'm far from a cow.

I turn my attention to Peyton to find her shooting daggers at Warner. My friend rarely holds her tongue. It seems we both choose to fight internally with his comment and disrespect for the Midwest.

Tired of the silence and lack of engagement by the guys, Warner speaks. "But if all of you want to go, I won't stand in your way."

"So, it's settled then," Carson concludes, smiling widely. "Meredith, I'll text you Corey's house manager's number, so you can arrange everything. We'll fly to L.A. today then to Iowa next week. Time to pack," he urges.

"You make a cute couple," Jake murmurs in passing, briefly touching my shoulder.

"If I'm sequestered in Iowa for months, I'm staying in Las Vegas for the week," Warner informs Meredith. "Make the arrangements; I'll be upstairs."

"I'm staying, too," Jake's gravelly voice adds as he walks out the door.

Meredith scowls. I'm not sure if it's the added task of extending their stay or the fear of the trouble they might cause with more time in Sin City. I hope she has to stay and babysit the two of them. As it's clear the woman isn't a fan of mine, I sort of hope the guys cause trouble and make her deal with it.

15

MONTANA

"With that settled," Peyton starts, "look at these photos I took last night."

Her fingers scroll through photo after photo. Unimpressed, Meredith leaves the room. Eli pauses beside Carson.

"Here." He places his palm flat upon Carson's chest. "It'll work. The two of you, I mean. Watch this, and you'll believe like we do." His index finger moves between Peyton and him.

When he pulls his palm from Carson's chest, I see he's given him a flash drive.

"What's this...?" Carson asks.

"It's a video of last night." Eli grins.

A video of our wedding. I'll need to thank him for recording it. As we can't remember, it's our only window into the ceremony, our vows, and our drunken behaviors last night.

"Can you send me the photos?" Carson asks Peyton. "Montana has my number."

It seems he's as eager as I am to relive last night.

"Watch the video. I'll head to our room and send the pics to Montana." Peyton hugs me before leaving. "Grab tissues; you'll need them, both of you." With that, she leaves the room.

"Where's your laptop?" I ask before the door latches behind Peyton.

He pulls his computer from a duffle near the head of the bed. Opening the lid, the machine sparks to life, and with a few keystrokes, he unlocks it. He inserts the flash drive into the port and opens it with a touch on his screen. He fiddles with the settings for sound and widescreen before looking to me to find out if I'm ready to watch our actions from last night.

Carson

"I'm ready." her voice cracks a little.

I take her right hand in mine, using my left to start the video.

Eli's videography skills are shaky, but I'll never mention it to him. I'll be forever grateful he thought to catch the moment on video.

He poses for a selfie with Peyton, the two laughing and talking animatedly about not believing what's about to happen. Next, he swings the camera to me standing near a small, raised altar I assume the man that waits with me is the officiant.

I'm standing tall, excited, and not swaying as I expected to be since I can't recall any of this.

"These are your last moments as a single man," Eli reminds me. "Any final thoughts?"

"What's taking her so long?" I mumble.

"Easy tiger," Eli attempts to settle my nerves. "She's wanting to make a grand entrance on this very important occasion. You can't fault her for that."

"I'll be fine when I see here," I growl. "I don't like her out of my sight."

Eli pats my shoulder, before taking his spot beside me and pointing the camera down the small aisle lined with a few white folding chairs.

The bridal march begins, the French doors open, and my heart stops.

Montana

I stare at Eli's video, Carson close at my side, still holding my hand in his. I watch myself walk down the aisle in a gorgeous, Marilyn Monroe style, white halter dress, the hem falling high on my thigh; my feet are adorned with delicate sandals and satin ribbons criss cross up my calves. The look is complete with the biggest smile I've ever worn.

My eyes lock upon Carson's while I make my way to his side. Eli turns the camera toward the men, then back to me as I assume my position beside Peyton who's still wearing her LBD.

Eli moves behind the officiant, framing the two of us in his lens. Occasionally, he zooms out to include Peyton in the video.

"You may exchange your own vows," the officiant states.

I look quickly to Carson, confused. *If we drank enough and we don't remember any of this, how were we able to say our own vows?* I prepare myself for drunken babble and slurring.

"Carson," I listen as I begin my vows, "I'll be the Oreos to your milk, holding you in my arms on a bad day. I promise to wear silk and to always come watch you play. I'll be beside you, no matter what life brings. I'll tickle your tattoos and always listen when you sing. I'll be your biggest fan, following wherever you lead. I'll do everything I can to be everything you need."

Wow. Where did I come up with those rhyming words? Did I spend an hour writing them? They're unique and express perfectly my new feelings for Carson.

He pauses the video. "How did you come up with your vows on the spot like that?" he asks me.

I raise his hand in mine and place it over my heart. He nods, gulping; I watch his Adam's apple move. He pushes play.

"I guess it's my turn," he says, looking to the official for confirmation. "My first, my last, my always. You're Leia to my Han Solo, Adrian to my Rocky, and my partner in crime. I promise to put the seat down, hold your hair back while you puke, and do my best to keep you safe. I'll strive to make you happy—I love your laugh. And, I'll make sure you never get locked out again."

I'm choked up, both on the video and now sitting beside him. His words, his beautiful and perfect words, fill my heart with joy.

Like me, he didn't seem drunk; he didn't even slur a single word. *So, why the hell can neither of us remember this special moment?*

We are pronounced husband and wife. Without prompting, I launch myself into Carson's arms; chest to chest, I wrap my arms around his neck and legs around his waist. His mouth crashes to mine; our lips battle, our bodies longing to show the vows we just shared.

It's not the wedding Peyton and I've planned a million times since our childhood; it's better. It's not traditional, and it's not scripted., It's spur of the moment with heartfelt honesty, just like our conversation on the floor of the hotel hallway the day before.

"Can we watch it again?" I ask.

He purses his lips, shaking his head. "We need to pack for the airport," Carson states. "We'll watch it again on the plane. Besides, Peyton is probably dying to have you to herself. I'll walk you to your room."

"It's about time," Peyton greets when I enter our room. "Did you watch the wedding video?"

"I can't believe how perfect it was," I explain. "Impromptu, honest, and perfect."

"I know, right?" she agrees. "Now, tell me. Do you really plan to stay married? I mean, last night I felt both of you knew exactly what you were doing, and it was meant to be. Now that I know neither of you remember it, and I assume that means you were drunk, I question your reasons to stay married."

"We're going to make it work," I reiterate. "We feel the same way we did last night, exchanging our vows. I can't explain it. It happened in an instant. There was no fighting love at first sight."

"Well, I guess I'll be flying back to Des Moines by myself." Peyton extends her lower lip out in a pout. "Some of us have a job to start in two days."

"Boo hoo," I mock. "At least you have a direction you are working towards. You know what you want. I'm still confused, even more so now. Speaking of confused, which guy did you end up choosing?" I wiggle my eyebrows at her.

"Guy?" she asks. "It's guys." She giggles.

My eyes grow to the size of saucers. *She can't mean... No, she wouldn't. Would she?*

"There's no need to choose. Men do it all the time. I chose both of them." She shows no remorse for her decision.

"And, they went for it?" I shouldn't ask; I don't want details, but I need to know where her mind is.

"It took some coaxing on my part," she blushes.

"I don't want details. I just need to know you are happy and safe."

"Happy is not the word for it. I'm sated for the moment. I had the best night of my life and hope to repeat it many times to come. Thanks to you, they'll be in Des Moines all summer."

"Peyton," fear laces my voice, "I'm afraid they'll hurt you. They're used to women throwing themselves at their feet every day. What will you do when they move on?"

"I'm not that vested in the relationship yet, so stop worrying. For now, I'm a single woman, having fun. It may be for a night or a few nights. I'm a big girl; I can take care of myself."

"So, while I got married in Vegas, you joined a thruple," I can't believe how our lives changed during our three days in Nevada.

"A thruple?" Peyton's brow furrows.

Unraveled

"Yes, a thruple. It's a threesome and a couple called a thruple. Or, do you prefer to use triad to describe it?"

"How do you know about this?" she asks, hands on her hips.

"I read romance novels, and I know things," I proudly state.

"Maybe you should start sharing your books with me," she teases. "I can't have you know more about my sexual conquests than I do."

"Crap! Look at the time," I screech. "We need to pack and be downstairs in an hour, and I still need to shower."

"Go shower; I'll pack for the both of us," she offers. "Just don't be surprised when some of your new clothes fly home with me today."

16

CARSON

In Los Angeles

"Montana, we're here," I murmur near her head which is resting on my shoulder. "It's time to wake up." I can't believe she didn't wake when we stopped at the security gate at the entrance to the neighborhood.

It warms my heart that she feels comfortable enough with me to sleep on my shoulder. We shared a long night of sex last night that neither of us remembers, and except holding hands while watching the wedding video, this is the first contact we've had since. My body craves her touch and loves having her near.

Her groggy eyes take a moment to focus on me before turning to my house.

"It's not the over-the-top mansion I thought it would be," she states, taking in my simple three-story beachfront house in Huntington Beach, CA.

"I'm not a mansion type of guy," I tell her. "Oh, fuck."

"Are those your...?"

"Yep. Those are my parents," I groan under my breath. "They're

Unraveled

supposed to be in San Diego." I turn to her. "I'm sorry; this is not what I planned."

I slide from the back seat, extending my arm for her to join me. I'm sure Mom heard about the wedding and nagged Dad until he drove her here to shut her up. This will be interesting; meet the parents, firing squad style.

We round the front of the black escalade before I see my new dog standing at Dad's side; I forgot he arrived this week. I stride toward my parents, more excited to meet my Malamute.

My mom, ever the sharp dresser, stands in her designer Velour tracksuit, complete with rhinestones and a word across her butt, in full makeup and high-heeled tennis shoes. My father's in his signature golf shirt and shorts with designer logos, brown leather loafers, and dark tan skin.

"Hello dear," Mom greets me, kissing each cheek European style.

"Mom," I hug her. "And, you come over here and meet your new daddy," I say to the furry beast near her feet.

"Who's this?" Montana bends to pet the friendly fur ball.

Untrained, the large puppy places his two enormous paws on her shoulders to lick her face, causing her to fall backward into the grass. Giggling, Montana shifts her face from side to side in an attempt to avoid licks, all the while rubbing the puppy's tummy above her.

I guess she's a dog lover. That's good since I forgot to discuss this with her before our arrival. So caught up in her, I completely forgot he'd arrive this week, and I would come home to my new companion instead of my lonely house.

"Okay, that's enough," I state. Pulling the mammoth fur ball from Montana's chest, I hand the red leash back to my dad.

Montana stands, brushing grass off of herself nervously, taking her place by my side.

"To what do I owe the honor?" I ask my mom.

"Well, dear," Mom answers, "we had a few free days and while reading the morning headlines, we were excited for you and wanted to speak with you before the band starts recording."

Crap! I neglected to introduce Montana right away. I pray she doesn't read into it. My parents caught me off guard, and I didn't mean to forget the introduction.

"Mom, Dad, this is my wife Montana." I smile proudly.

Montana smiles back at me; we both realize it's the first time I've called her my wife.

"Montana, this is my dad and mom, Kurt and Aaron."

I watch nervously as Mom's eyes assess her. She has her feelers out; she wants to start the interrogation and be nosey, but she waits. This may be the longest evening ever.

Montana

In a whirlwind, I meet Carson's new puppy and his parents. I know Carson didn't plan for company when we arrived in L.A. I roll with it because, as a newly married couple, we are bound to be ambushed by our parents, siblings, and friends.

When we entered the house, Carson wanted to take me on a tour, but Aaron announced they had supper ready and sent Carson's housekeeper home early, promising to care for the puppy until we arrived. This doesn't please my new husband.

"Carson, help your father fetch the meat off the grill," his mom orders. "Montana, you can help me place these on the patio table." She motions to salad and dishes on the kitchen counter, and I comply.

"What is it you do?" Aaron asks, as soon the men are out of earshot.

"I recently graduated from a community college with my Associate's Degree," I explain. "I'm deciding this summer if I'll head back to school or find a job."

"So, you're taking a gap year? That's convenient." His mother raises her eyebrows.

Is she insinuating I did not meet Carson by chance?

Unraveled

"What do your parents do for a living?" she continues as she hands me two bowls and signals for me to follow her out another set of doors to a patio table.

"My father owns a large farm north of Des Moines, and my mother runs the family's real estate business. They also own several properties."

After we place the dishes in the center of the table, I follow her back indoors.

"Any desire to go into the family business?" she queries.

I shake my head. Although I'm not sure what career I'd like, I do know it's not farming or real estate. I've helped both of my parents off and on throughout the years. I respect what they do; it's just not for me.

Aaron stands with her hands on her hips. "He's seldom home. What do you plan to do while he's away?"

"I guess that's what I'll be deciding this summer," I reply. "I could work toward my bachelor's degree or work full time by fall. I just don't know yet."

"How'd you pay for the Las Vegas trip with no job?" she pries.

Carson

Dad and I enter the kitchen in time to hear Montana defending herself.

"Not that I owe you an explanation," she remains calm. "When I was 18, my brother and I created an app. We sold it a year later to a tech company for close to six million dollars. I also have a small trust fund when I turn 25, and I own 10 percent of my family's real estate business. Trust me; your son's money is safe."

"Mom, that's enough," I demand, raising my voice. "I won't have you attack her when I turn my back."

"Uh, what?" Mom feigns innocence.

"You need to trust that I know what I'm doing and accept Montana as my wife and your daughter-in-law. Or, we won't welcome you in our house."

Montana places her hand upon my shoulder. "It's fine, Carson. I'm sure my parents would worry about the same things if our roles were reversed."

I kiss her temple, placing my arm around her shoulders, escorting her with me to the patio.

During dinner, it's as if nothing happened; we eat steaks, salad, and asparagus with wine and water. Montana's stories and our questions about the city of Des Moines, her family, and her brother's African adventures keep us entertained.

"Finish your wine," I urge Montana and Dad. "I'll help Mom with the dishes."

We load our arms with the empty dishes and make our way inside. While I load the dishwasher, Mom moves leftovers into containers and places them into the refrigerator.

"Tell me how you met," Mom instructs.

"It's like the opposite of the Big Bang theory," I explain. "With us, instead of the collision of the two objects exploding outwards, the explosion happened inside. When we met, it's like we collided, and a fire lit within me. Our meeting, our collision, sparked a reaction here." I point to my chest. "The more we talked, the more we were together, the fire grew and flowed through my veins. Call it love at first sight, fate, destiny, or blind luck, but it happened within two days. I'm all in; I'm a goner. Cupid's arrow permanently pierces my heart. I am in love."

Mom chuckles. "Your descriptions are verbose and vivid. You could have said 'I knew it the moment I saw her.'"

I could have, but that isn't adequate for the physical and chemical reaction between us. We aren't the typical "boy meets girl, boy dates girl, boy marries girl" story. We are much more than that.

17

MONTANA

With our empty wine glasses in hand, Kurt and I join the others in the kitchen, Denali, the Malamute, trotting behind us.

"Let me give Montana a tour, then we can meet on the rooftop," Carson suggests to his parents.

"So, this is the kitchen." He swings his arms wide.

I'm already very familiar with this open space, with the large island with seating for five, and the bar area to the side, near the floor-to-ceiling glass doors, leading to the outdoor grill.

A few steps away, also on the first floor, we walk through a giant living room, complete with a wall of glass, two French doors to the patio where we ate, a small powder room, and a mudroom with a shower off to the patio side.

Near the table where we ate, the stone patio holds a wicker sectional with large, cushioned chairs, a glass railing all around, and a glass gate that opens to a wooden ramp which leads down to the private beach he promises to show me tomorrow.

Next, he ushers me upstairs to find an open seating area, three bedrooms and three baths with French doors onto a balcony off of the seating area.

On the third floor, he shows me a library at the top of stairs, French doors to yet another large balcony, and more stairs that continue to the roof. Before we climb, he opens two heavy wooden doors, unveiling his master bedroom and bath, the largest walk-in closet I've ever stood in, and his personal library space. He tugs me from the room much too soon.

We continue up the stairs to find patio chairs and tables, string lights, large planters with tropical plants, a putting green, and a fabulous view of the sandy beach and ocean below. His parents sip from wine glasses, sitting around a stone table with a fire burning in its center.

"We brought up the wine and the puppy," Carson's father boasts.

We enjoy our drinks on the rooftop patio, sitting in chaise loungers with throw blankets to ward off the cool ocean breeze. His parents decide to shop and eat at a quaint beachfront dive bar they frequent when in town. They invite the two of us to join them tomorrow. An hour passes before his parents excuse themselves for bed.

Carson

"Where would you like to sleep?" I ask, nervous of her answer.

She shrugs beneath her blanket, a small smile gracing her lips.

I continue. "How about we take Denali out for a potty break then chat in my room until you're ready to sleep?"

She nods, a smile growing larger. Standing, she folds her blanket before placing it on the seat.

"We should grab a snack, too," she hints. "Can Denali sleep in your room tonight with us?"

I shake my head, smiling. This woman can have anything she asks for. I'm putty in her hand.

After eating a snack of cheese and crackers, Montana takes Denali out front to potty while I move the dog paraphernalia to my room. I had no idea puppies needed this much stuff.

Unraveled

Montana

I struggle to find a patch of grass or dirt out front for Carson's puppy to do its business. I never knew grass to be a luxury; I take it for granted in Iowa. Lucky for the both of us, Denali is a male. He lifts his leg and waters a lamppost near the end of the driveway. Thank heavens he didn't need to go number two. *I wonder if Denali will fly with us or remain in L.A.*

Later, in bed chatting, I keep looking at the puppy in the kennel on the floor in the corner of Carson's room. It seems cruel to place him in a cage while we are here. I realize he might chew on things, but with us near, he can't do any damage.

"If this were my house," I blurt, "Denali would sleep with me."

He hops from his side of the bed, frees Denali from the cage, and helps him up onto the bed. The large fur ball licks my cheek then lumbers to Carson's side and lays lengthways beside him. While I rub his belly and pet his head, he licks my arm and cheek before yawning.

"It's your house too," Carson informs me. "In California, what's mine is yours in our marriage."

With that, our conversation turns to our arrangement and the important items we should know about each other. We talk financials; I share in further detail the app I created and sold. He's surprised when I tell him it's the casino map and friend tracking app I downloaded to his phone. I share that we split the earnings 70 percent mine as it was my idea and I did most of the research, 15 percent my brother's, and 15 percent to the coder we hired.

I wake the next morning alone in Carson's bed. We talked until the wee hours of the morning last night. In fact, I'm not sure if I fell asleep first or if he did. I learned about his parent's house, his father's marketing firm, and his brother and sister. Looking around the room, I notice Denali is missing as well.

In his bathroom, I run my fingers through my hair and wash my face. My reflection tells me I'm presentable, so I head downstairs for breakfast. From the bottom step, I see breakfast is spread out on the island, buffet-style.

I smile, waving at Carson's house manager. He told me all about her last night. She's a single mom named Sonny with a four-year-old son, Matt. I find he sits, coloring, while nibbling on his breakfast.

Sonny stands behind the island, wearing a warm smile, dressed casually.

"Good morning," I greet, taking a plate. I butter toast then spread peanut butter on top. I place fresh fruit and yogurt on my plate then sit by the little boy.

"I like your picture. Can you tell me about it?" I encourage.

Matt points to parts of the drawing and tells me about it. Soon, Carson's parents join us to eat.

"Is Carson still asleep?" his mother asks, taking the barstool beside me.

Sonny answers before I can admit I have no clue where he is.

"Carson took Denali on a walk at the beach." She looks at her watch. "He left 20 minutes ago and should be back soon."

My plate empty, I place it in the dishwasher, much to Sonny's protest.

"I think I'll venture to the beach," I state, walking to the patio door.

I find the pair right away. Carson's private beach is a quarter of a mile long. Carson greets me with a kiss on my cheek. Denali greets me with large, wet paws to my thighs. My husband informs me they've walked back and forth several times.

"He needs obedience school," Carson mutters. "He shouldn't jump up like that."

"How old is he? Six weeks?" I defend. "He needs stability. You'll just have to train him and reward him with little treats."

Unraveled

"We," Carson interjects. "*We* will train him; *we* will give him stability."

I nod. It's hard to remember we are a couple; what's his is mine and mine is his. Having only had two serious relationships lasting two months, I'm not practiced in referring to myself as part of a pair.

We walk the dog three more laps on the beach.

"Your housekeeper seems nice, and her son is too adorable. How long has she worked for you? And how does she make it by only working part time?"

Carson informs me, "She's my house manager, not housekeeper. She lives in the mother-in-law suite above the garage. I didn't show that to you as I didn't want to disturb her last night. She works for me all year, and I provide benefits. I even pay for Matt's preschool nearby."

We turn around and head back in the direction we just came from.

He continues, "She once mentioned to me that I should open the house to be an Airbnb while I'm touring. I gave her permission to do that and allow her to keep those profits. I can't lose her, so I try to spoil her like she spoils me."

We return to the house, towel drying Denali's paws before we enter.

"Oh my, look at the time," I urge. "We're supposed to head out with your parents in an hour. I'll take Denali to his kennel, and you get in the shower."

Carson pulls me against his chest. I feel him vibrate as his husky voice invites, "If we shower together, we can save time."

I raise an eyebrow, unsure if I'm ready for showering together.

He smiles his sexy smirk.

The next morning, while eating breakfast, my phone vibrates, signaling a FaceTime call. "Excuse me; I need to take this." I scoot my chair from the breakfast table and Carson's parents.

"It's my brother," I whisper to Carson as I pass.

"Hello," I greet nervously, aware of the lecture coming my way.

"I didn't wake you, did I?" Joe asks.

"We're eating breakfast. It's eight here," I answer. "What time is it in Africa?"

"About five. We're getting ready for dinner," he explains.

In the background, I see bare dirt and huts in the distance.

"I miss you," I whisper, fighting back my tears.

"I'm sure you do, but we've got other stuff to cover." My brother's voice takes on an authoritative tone. "What were you thinking?"

"Joe..." Tears fall, and my throat swells shut.

"Let's put aside the fact that you were blitzed in an unfamiliar city with strangers that are rock stars. Mom says you're not getting the annulment. Montana, you can't stay married to a complete stranger. Who does that?" He pauses for a moment. "Insane people, that's who."

"Joe, he's not a stranger." I clear my throat in the hopes my voice sounds serious. "I know we rushed the wedding, but we're slowing things down now."

"That's the craziest thing I've ever heard. He could be a serial killer, a rapist, a deadbeat loser, an abusive S.O.B.--"

"I know you're upset with me," I interrupt his list. "But it upsets me that you think so little of me."

"Montana, that's not what I meant," he quickly clarifies. "You've always been level-headed. I never thought in a million years you'd elope in Vegas. Peyton, yes—you, never."

"Did Mom tell you we spent two days together? And that there were instantly signs this wasn't only attraction?" I swallow, then quickly continue. "If it were someone I met hours before marrying, I would have annulled. Carson's different. We spent a lot of time together, and I couldn't bear the thought of leaving Las Vegas and never seeing him again. We're just going to spend some time together. If it doesn't work out, then we'll get a divorce. We both felt it's worth trying to stay together."

"You expect me to believe in two days you knew enough to marry this guy?" Joe asks.

"Joe, we both agree Carson and I rushed into marriage. Two days is *not* enough time to make the commitment," I explain. "We are interested enough that we didn't want to go our separate ways without trying, though. I believe in love at first sight. When he sat beside me in the hotel hallway and we made small talk, there was an instant connection. I felt complete for the first time. We spent that evening together with Peyton and his band. He never once tried to hold my hand or kiss me. We talked and talked and talked. He's different from any guy I've ever crushed on or dated. You'll see."

I position myself on the patio chair. "I wish you were in the States. Then, you'd see he's all I say he is and more. We're headed to Iowa tomorrow. I can't wait for Mom and Dad to meet him."

A little boy packing a heavy pail walks close behind Joe. He's adorable, all dusty in a much-to-big t-shirt and bare feet. I'd hoped to visit my brother in Africa this summer. His village in the background of our calls entices me. My trip to Africa will need to wait. I married Carson and need to invest my time in our relationship.

"You know they'll rake him over the coals," Joe warns.

"I'm very aware of that."

"If I were in Iowa, this never would have happened. What kind of brother lets his little sister elope with a rock star?" He shakes his head, his scraggly brown hair flying everywhere in the breeze.

"The only way you'd have prevented it was not allowing me to go to Las Vegas with Peyton. And, we both know you wouldn't have been able to stop Peyton's girls' trip."

"Get an annulment; then, you can date him if you want him in your life. You can't stay married to him," my big brother orders. "An annulment or a divorce. Take your pick."

"Joe, I need you to hear me," I bite. "I love him. We're staying married, so deal with it."

I've never spoken to my brother like this. In fact, I've never been this mad or disappointed in him. I understand he's trying to protect me, but this is my decision; I'm a grown woman. If he can't accept my decision, then it's a good thing he's halfway around the world in Africa.

"Are those waves I'm hearing?" Joe's smile signals he's done with his big-brother lecture.

I turn the camera, sharing the beach view.

"Damn! Mom didn't tell me his house is on the beach," Joe chuckles.

"Yeah, well, Mom doesn't know much... yet." I chuckle. "Other than being on the beach, his house is pretty normal."

I rise from my patio chair, giving him a 360-degree view.

"That's way too much glass to be a *normal* house. Nice try," he teases.

"I meant on the inside," I explain. "It's casual, not flashy or formal. His parents are here, or I'd take you on a tour."

Joe turns his stance, and more of the village comes into view. Now, I see a group of school-age children sitting around a woman with a guitar on the steps to the medical tent. The children clap and wiggle with her music.

"Who's that?" I ask, not recognizing her from the staff I've met in his previous video calls.

"She's the musician I've mentioned before. When she's free, she visits with her music. She encourages them to trust the doctors." Something's different in his voice, but I don't press the subject. I'm proud of the work he does for Doctors Without Borders. Selling my app allowed him to volunteer. Instead of working exhausting hours at a hospital to pay off his student loans, he graduated debt free with money left over to volunteer in under-privileged regions.

"They look so happy." My eyes stay on the children. "Are they still teaching you to play soccer?"

"Yes, and I'm still pretending to suck at it," he laughs. "They enjoy teaching me and laugh at my mess-ups."

The woman, finished with her song, stands, waves to the children, then walks towards my brother. He quickly places the camera back on his face.

"She's gorgeous." I tell him something he already knows.

Unraveled

"Shh. She's coming this way." I can barely hear his low voice. "I'll let you go."

I'm surprised by his sudden desire to disconnect.

"I love you, and I miss you," I state before saying goodbye.

"Montana, be careful. I'd hate to fly home and kick his butt if he hurts you. I might wind up in jail." He winks and smirks at me.

I hold my phone tight to my chest. With his closing words, Joe's letting me live my life and offering his support. I'm confident that when my family meets Carson, they'll understand.

18

CARSON

At Des Moines International Airport

Montana directs our driver to take us to the end of the terminal for the rental car counters. Since Peyton picked up her vehicle last week when she flew home while we went to L.A., I'm renting a vehicle today for me and the guys to use for the summer. I select a sweet, red, Jeep Wrangler Rubicon Recon 4x4. I can't wait to take the doors and top off.

"Should we stop and grab a few things on our way to Corey's house?" she asks as we pull from the airport.

"No, we'll get back out later if we need to," I promise, ready to get to the house and relax.

Montana helps me navigate through the city; then, we let our GPS guide us to the house. She also texts her mother and Peyton that we are safe in Des Moines and makes plans to talk tomorrow.

At the security gate I buzz, give my name, and we drive up the long, winding lane. Standing outside the front door are two women to greet us.

"You didn't tell me Miss Kelly would be here," Montana's voice is high-pitched, excited, and she hops from the jeep before I can get out myself. "Miss Kelly!" she calls, arms wide, walking to her.

"Oh my Lord, Montana, what are you doing here?" the woman who I assume is Miss Kelly asks, walking to hug Montana.

"Carson Cavanaugh, ma'am," I greet, extending my hand.

"Phish!" Kelly waves off my greeting. "It's Kelly, not ma'am."

"So, how do the two of you know each other?" I query.

"I've known Montana since she was knee high to a grasshopper," Kelly answers.

"My mom serves on several charity boards with Miss Kelly," Montana explains.

"Let me make proper introductions," Kelly states. "I'm Corey's mother, Kelly, and this is Corey's house manager, Fran. She'll see to anything and everything you might need while you are here."

Montana

Corey's house is not the mansion I assumed it to be. It's a large house for the Des Moines area but looks similar to many other houses in design. As we follow Miss Kelly and Fran into the home, we find the decor is comfy and relaxed with lots of photos of his family, friends, and other entertainers. Adding to this inviting interior are large pillows, overstuffed cushions, and hardwood floors, not the cold tile many prestigious mansions would boast. The space looks lived in rather than uninviting.

19

MONTANA

The Next Morning

Carson and I sleep in until Denali signals he needs to potty by licking my face to wake me up. We hook him to the leash and head out on a long walk near the lake. Since we won't be leaving Corey's property, I keep on the t-shirt and boxers I wore to bed last night.

We laugh at Denali's attempt to lift his back leg to wet on everything over six inches tall.

"No way he has more urine left to mark with," I giggle.

"Don't make fun of him!" Carson acts offended. "He's a growing boy, trying to make his mark on the world."

"What is it with males of every species needing to pee as many places as possible? My brother used to pee on Mom's plants in the backyard and everywhere on Dad's farm," I share.

"Not all of us pee everywhere," Carson defends.

"Ever peed in the snow?" I raise my eyebrow in his direction. At his nod, I continue, "Go on a tree?"

"Okay; some of us go outside once or twice in our lifetime," he admits.

"Only twice? I call bullshit."

Unraveled

We've reached the lake, so I lead Denali to the water's edge. He stops with his front two paws in the water; his head low, he laps up as much water as he can.

"Poor thing dehydrated himself walking down here," Carson deadpans.

I laugh loudly at Carson's words and the loud lapping of water by Denali.

"Let's sit on the dock," Carson suggests, and I follow, tugging the leash behind me.

At first, Denali's scared to walk on the wooden dock as it moves with the gentle waves. I kneel beside him. "It's okay," I coo, patting for him to step towards me. "C'mon, that's it."

Within arm's length, I praise him with belly rubs and strokes under his chin. "You're a brave boy. Yes, you are."

Carson chuckles behind me. I look over my shoulder at him, blocking the bright sun with my free hand. Carson smashes his teeth between his lips, moving his fingers as if zipping his mouth shut before tossing the imaginary key over his shoulder. He can make fun of my baby-talking to Denali all he likes. Soon, he'll do it, too.

I rise, pulling the fluffy puppy with me to the end of the dock. I slip off my shoes, dipping my foot in the water below. I pat the board beside me, inviting Carson to join me.

As the two of us sit, gently kicking our bare feet in the cool lake water, Denali, who's seated beside me, whimpers. His front paws are inches from the edge. He leans his nose towards the water then whines again.

"It's okay," I promise, placing my hand in the water in front of him.

He steps up, closer to the edge. When he lowers his head, I swirl my hand in the water in front of him. He watches my movements closely. With no warning, he jumps into the lake, splashing the two of us.

Carson laughs while I freak out. *What if he can't swim?* It's his first time in a lake. Tears well in my eyes as my fear grows.

"Atta boy," Carson cheers, turning to watch Denali paddle to shore.

I attempt to wipe my tears, hiding them from him. My breathing calms while I watch Denali shake himself dry on shore. I take in a deep breath now that he's safely on land.

"What's wrong?" Carson asks, pulling me into his embrace.

I sniffle, shaking my head, not looking up to meet his eyes. He lifts my chin, forcing me to let him see my tears.

"Were you scared?"

I nod. "What if he couldn't swim?" I whimper, my voice unsteady.

"Honey, he can swim," he chuckles. "He did the doggie paddle."

I giggle at him. I turn quickly in his arms at the loud splash as Denali jumps in from the deck again.

"He's okay. No need to worry. He's okay." Carson's calm voice soothes me. "I'm not sure how we'll get him out of the water to go eat breakfast, though," Carson chuckles. "You're protective of him; I like that." His lips hover near mine. "I love you."

My breath catches, and my fingers clutch tight to his t-shirt. Those three words catch me off guard. Three little words, eight letters; they are powerful. They're heady. We're married; we should love each other. "I love you," he said with me in his arms, sharing a simple, private moment. He beat me to it; he said it first. He loves me.

Back at the house, I dart into the shower before I eat breakfast. When I descend the stairs and enter the kitchen, Miss Kelly points to the security screen. My mom waits at the gate. Miss Kelly enters the code and urges her to drive on up to the house.

"I need to pop into the restroom; I'll be right back," I tell her.

When I return, I hear Mom and Miss Kelly chatting excitedly as they enter the house. While they catch up on the many charity boards and activities they are involved in, I sneak out back with Denali for a minute.

I walk closer to the studio door while Denali looks for the best place to lift his leg. Although the urge to open the door and peek

Unraveled

inside is strong, I fight it. Carson needs to work, and I have plans with Mom. Denali finishes, and we walk back inside.

"I thought you were going to text me when you were at the gate," I remind Mom. "Miss Kelly, you want to join us for lunch?"

"No, thank you," she answers. "I'm running errands; I just popped by to make sure you had everything you need. I have too much to do today while the dogs are at the groomers."

"Let's eat," Mom suggests, placing her arm around my shoulders and waving to her friend.

"Want to meet Carson before we go?" I ask, hopeful and wanting a reason to be near him.

"No, let's wait until after we eat," Mom suggests. "We have a ton to talk about."

"A ton." That's an understatement. I'm not sure exactly what my mom's reaction is and am sure she has much to lecture me about.

Mom is unusually quiet as we drive down the long lane from Corey's house. I find the silence unbearable.

"In the mood for Gilroy's?" I ask nervously.

"Ooh, I love that place," Mom states. "Is that on 8th Street?"

"Yes; we can sit on the patio and drink Moscow mules with lunch," I add. "Mom, let's start our conversation now, so we can enjoy lunch."

"We'll enjoy lunch, no matter what," Mom declares. "This lunch isn't to punish you, Montana. We have a lot of questions and answers to cover."

"So, shall I tell you about him?" The urge to start our talk grows with every silent, passing moment.

"First, I have something to tell you," Mom opens.

I swallow hard. Here we go. Here's the disappointment statement. Here's the guilt trip.

"When you won at your slot machine..." Mom begins. "The woman, Dawn, in the photograph you posted on social media..."

This is nowhere near what I expected her to say. I thought she'd lecture me on responsibility and the sanctity of marriage.

"Dawn and I serve on the JDRF and Variety Club boards together." Mom smiles at me before returning her eyes to the road. "It's a small world, isn't it?"

"Yes," I agree. "She told me she was from Des Moines. In fact, she asked if she could text me a photo of us to sneakily get my cell number. Then, she mentioned I'd be perfect for one of her single sons."

"She's out of luck on that matter, now, isn't she?" Mom laughs. "Married women can't go on blind dates."

"Hmm, I hadn't thought of that," I lie. "Guess that means you can't keep setting me up then, too."

As we laugh together, my mood lightens, and my worries fade. The dread I had for this lunch disappears.

After we order our drinks, Mom adjusts the umbrella to better block the sun from our faces then starts her list of questions. "So, how did you meet?"

I share the story of being locked out of the room, waiting on the hall floor for the maintenance staff, and how Carson nearly stepped on me.

"You'll be happy to know he's polite, not only to me but to everyone around him," I promise.

"He's handsome," Mom giggles.

"Duh! Of course, he's handsome." *Did she expect me to settle down with an ogre? I mean, I'm not superficial or vain, but I do have 20/20 vision.*

"He's a regular guy. Good values and family are important to him," I share. "Sparks flew the instant we met, and although we were impulsive on our second night out, it's both our family values that has us staying together instead of signing for a quick annulment."

While we nibble on our shared appetizer then our meal, I continue telling Mom about the band, Carson's writer's block, the lyrics he's started writing, and how he changed their plan to record in Des Moines instead of L.A. to be near me. "Here." I hand her my cell phone, open to photos I took of his house.

"I can't wait for you to see his beach house in person. The photos don't do it justice. Keep scrolling," I prompt.

"That's his house manager, Sonny, and her son, Matt," I state. "She lives on the premises, and he keeps her on full-time, all year-round. She had the idea to rent his home out as an Airbnb while he's on tour. Because it was her idea, he lets her keep all the money she earns from that."

"Wow," Mom reacts with a mouth full of food.

"He treats her like family. It's sweet," I confirm.

"You look radiant," Mom blurts. "He's good for you."

"Mom…"

"What are we waiting for? Let's go so I can meet my new son-in-law," Mom says, waving for our bill.

"Lunch is on me," I state. When Mom argues, I inform her, "I won even more money on my second day in Las Vegas."

Smiling, she shakes her head.

On the ride back to Saylorville Lake, I decide to ask my mom for advice. "What was it like being married to Dad in the beginning?"

Mom shares about nerves, getting to know everything about each other, about marriage, and trust. She tells me she protects Dad as much as he protects her. She hurts when he does, celebrates when he does. Marriage is a work in progress, and so is love. It's not all desire, and it's based on loyalty.

"I feel like a middle school girl with a crush," I share. "I want to be near him twenty-four-seven, and I can't stop thinking about him; I'm like a bee, constantly buzzing around him. My heart constantly pounds my ribcage."

"That's the early stages of love," Mom assures me. "The honeymoon phase isn't just a weekend or week. It's a year or two. It's hard, but you need to find your own identity, even as his wife. You can't lose yourself in him, or you'll never last."

I nod.

"I know you planned to decide this summer whether to continue with college or find a job of interest to you," Mom says. "Is that still your plan?"

I nod again. "I'm leaning more towards entrepreneurship. But I'm not 100 percent sure yet."

"Well, you've proven yourself in that arena already with your app," Mom agrees. "I think you could make a go of it."

"I have a product I've been working with Peyton on," I share. "Maybe I'll use the summer to give it legs and see if I'm happy while doing it."

"Sounds like a brilliant plan," Mom states, pressing the call button at the gate.

Carson

As Fran opens the gate, my nerves skyrocket. Montana promised me her mother will come around quicker than my mom did. She describes her as positive and always smiling. But she's never eloped with a rock star before. She has no way of knowing how her parents will react to our marriage. My hands shake as I reach to open the front door.

"Carson," Montana calls as she jogs towards me. "This is my mom, Tony. Mom, this is Carson Cavanaugh, my husband."

I smile at Montana and her words before I turn to greet her mother.

"Mrs. Randall, it's a pleasure. Come, let's sit." I motion to the interior of the house.

"We'll have none of that," Mrs. Randall orders.

Crap! She's not happy with me or the marriage. Bloody hell, this will be a long afternoon.

"You'll call me Tony," she states. "Mrs. Randall was my mother-in-law." She laughs at what I'm sure is the scared look upon my face.

"Okay," I agree. "Tony, please join us inside."

Montana's mother walks ahead of us. I look to Montana with raised brows. She shakes her head, an enormous smile upon her face. She mouths, "Everything is good." Her words do little to settle my nerves.

"Mom, would you like a drink?" Montana asks before we take a seat.

"Yes, tea or water please," Tony replies.

"Would you like to sit here in the living room, out on the pool deck, or in the kitchen?" I ask.

"We ate on the patio, and it's heating up," Tony informs me. "Let's find a spot in the kitchen."

I motion for her to follow the steps her daughter took only moments before, and I follow. We sit at the kitchen island, and Montana places ice-cold drinks in front of each of us.

"Carson," Tony begins, "Montana has told me so much about you today. It's nice to meet you."

"Thanks," I respond. "I hope most of it was good."

"Phish." Tony waves her hand. "Seems you're much more than a rock star."

20

MONTANA

Late that Night

Nestled in the warmth of our king-sized bed, Carson cuddles my back against his front for several long moments as we talk.

Tonight, I pull away, lying on my side to face him. The pale moonlight allows me to see his face. Too many thoughts clog my mind.

What if we have no sexual chemistry in the bedroom, if we're not compatible sexually? Will our marriage and friendship end? What if he has terrible habits that I can't bear? What will happen if I want to go back to college or start my career in Des Moines? What if his writer's block returns? What if I snore?

"What's going on in there?" Carson taps my forehead before tucking hair behind my ear.

"There's still so much we don't know about each other," I admit. It's not a lie; I'm summing up all of my concerns.

He nods. "Let's remedy that now."

I scrunch my face, unsure what he means. *How can we remedy it now?*

"Do you have any allergies," Carson inquires.

"Chocolate makes me itch with hives. You?"

"I'm allergic to bees," he shares. "I carry an EpiPen everywhere I go." His hand brushes lightly over my cheek then falls between us. "How old were you when you first tried alcohol? And, what was it?" He smiles.

I guess we're playing twenty questions to learn more about each other.

"I was 16 at a party at Peyton's house while her parents were out of town," I answer. "I'm not sure what it was. I suspect it was a punch of sorts. Red liquid in red cups. There were so many bottles around the concoction, it could have been any or all of them." I raise my eyebrows. "You?"

"I was 16--"

"Uh-huh," I interrupt. "You can't use my answer. Tell the truth."

"I'm trying to," he defends. "I was 16; I snuck a bottle of vodka from my parents' liquor cabinet. Eli and I drank the entire bottle during our band practice. This was before Jake and Warner joined us."

"How'd you get that scar?" I point to his left jaw.

His fingers trace the jagged scar as if he'd forgotten he had it. "A broken beer bottle, pulling Jake and Warner from a bar fight when we were 19."

I'm not surprised he protected his bandmates then, just like he does today. It's one of the endearing qualities that drew me to him.

"What were you like in middle school and high school?" he queries.

"I was a nerd of sorts," I begin. *Why is describing myself so difficult?*

"I read a lot, took advanced-placement courses, took part in clubs and sports. But my genuine passion was to hole up in my room, reading, writing in my journal, or researching online." I shrug. "I was boring, really."

"What did you read?"

"In middle school, mostly John Greene and Stephen King…"

"That rhymes," he chortles.

"In high school," I continue, rubbing my tired eyes, "I discovered true crime and romance novels." I blush, hoping the faint moonlight hides my pink cheeks. "Online, I binged TED Talks, documentaries, conspiracy theories, and STEM related articles."

"Diverse. I like it." Carson repositions himself on his two fluffy pillows, body still turned to face me.

"Let me guess." I bite my lips as I contemplate a younger version of Carson. "You were a jock, captain of sports teams, before you gave it all up to start a band with Eli. It became your addiction, and you became successful."

He smirks, "I played sports all the way through high school, even when we started the band. I was the typical SoCal teen, hanging at the beach, surfing, and skateboarding, anything to be outside. It wasn't until Jake joined the band that I gave everything up for my music. Hmm..." he pauses to think. "What's your favorite food?"

I don't even have to think about it. "Peanut butter," I share. "All things peanut related are my favorite."

"I'm a potato junkie," Carson tells me. "All shapes and forms of potatoes. What's your favorite color?"

This really is twenty questions. It's working; we are learning about each other.

"That's a tough one," I confess. "I'm partial to blues, everything from Carolina blue to royal blue. But I also like to wear a lot of black." I struggle to get the last part of my answer out through my yawn.

"That's enough for tonight. We're tired," Carson states.

"Just one more," I plead before another yawn. "Who's your hero? Or someone you look up to?"

The corners of his eyes crinkle with his gigantic smile. "It's corny, and you'll judge me."

I cross my finger over my heart. "I promise no judgement if you'll tell me why that person is your hero."

"President Bill Clinton," he blurts then waits for my reaction.

I do my best to keep my eyes from widening and my jaw from falling open.

Carson explains, "He's the first President I was old enough to remember. We learned about him in grade school, and my parents did a magnificent job of keeping me from hearing about the Monica Lewinsky scandal. For much of my life, he was a great President. I love the tone of his voice. It draws others to listen; it's melodic."

"No judgement," I whisper, fighting sleep no more.

Carson

After that, we lie in bed each night, talking about anything and everything. We talk until we can no longer keep our eyes open, then wake the next morning, cuddling each other. We bare our souls, sharing every part of us. It's intimate. For now, it's the only intimacy we share.

We share about our siblings and what it was like growing up. I grind my teeth when she tells me about dating in high school, attending dances, and losing her virginity.

We share our most embarrassing moments, worst and best dates, and even our first broken heart.

I tell her about the vacations I shared with my family, and she tells me about those with her parents and Peyton. We were both in scouts, and neither of us has a tattoo. We even share the same fear that we do not understand how to be a husband and a wife. With all that we've shared at night, we've so much more to learn about each other.

As much as I love writing lyrics and playing music, I look forward to our nightly talks and waking in each other's arms. It's simple; it's sweet. But it's causing me to need the rest of her. I long for her to give herself over to me completely, the way we did on our wedding night, although we don't remember it.

21

CARSON

Days Later

"Are you ready for this?" I ask Montana. "These are the last few minutes of having the house all to ourselves. Our peace will be no more."

"The house is enormous—plenty of room to spread out," Montana reminds me.

Moments later, we're snacking in the kitchen when the gate buzzes, signaling the band's arrival.

Montana asks, "Fran, are you ready for this?"

She nods. "Corey's family and ZipTie have prepared me for everything."

When we open the front door to greet the guys, the first person I see is a label representative, giving orders into his Bluetooth earpiece and barking orders to the younger male hovering nearby.

Eli, our drummer, is the first through the door, two duffels in his hands, Jake the bass player, strolls in sans luggage. They take in the foyer and stairs. Eli smirks at Montana. "How's the married life, child bride?" Turning to me, he chuckles. "She looks happy; atta boy."

"She's not a child," I defend.

"Where's Warner?" she asks.

"Said he'd rather play in L.A. and not fuck cows in Iowa," Eli shares.

"Warner will arrive in two more days," the label rep informs as he lays down his next set of bags.

"Pompous ass," Jake mutters on his way back out to the SUV. He returns with a small travel kennel in his hand and a diaper bag in his other. "Eli, this isn't a 5-star hotel. Unload your own crap."

Eli jogs over. "Snoopy, are you ready to escape that nasty cage? I bet you are ready to pee on everything sticking up in the backyard, aren't ya?"

I'm thankful we thought to put Denali in his kennel in our bedroom. Eli didn't tell us he planned to bring Snoopy, his Jack Russell Terrier. It shouldn't be an issue. The house is plenty big enough for all of us, and it will give Denali someone to play with while we work.

"That's everything from the Escalade," the rep tells us. "You've got our numbers if you've forgotten anything, need anything, or... well... you know." He shuts the door behind him, evidently eager to head back to the small Des Moines airport and the west coast.

"Since it's not the Ritz, can you help us carry our bags to our rooms?" Eli asks, walking up the stairs with Snoopy and his paraphernalia.

Jake has his over-sized duffle on his back and picks up Eli's two bags, muttering on his way. "Which room?"

"The first on the left is ours, and the door is closed," I tell both of them. "The other four bedroom doors are open; pick your own."

"There's one more master suite at the end of the hall," Montana informs. "Since Warner's not here, one of you should take it. That'll teach him to dis on Iowa." She giggles at her own orneriness.

"Meet in the kitchen in five minutes," I call to the guys. "Bring Snoopy; I'll go over some house rules."

"Fran," Montana calls out as she enters the kitchen area. She disappears in the large walk-in pantry. "I'm gonna set out a few beers for the guys and some chips."

"I can do it." Fran quickly attempts to get between Montana and her task.

"No, I've got it. You'll keep busy come mealtimes," Montana reminds her. "Besides, I need something to keep me busy."

"I can't believe Warner's not here," Montana tells me when she re-enters the kitchen. "Our nightlife doesn't compare to Las Vegas or Los Angeles, but we still have fun. Peyton and I will show the four of you fun in Iowa. What are we going to do about the dogs?" she asks.

"Dogs?" Eli asks, entering the room, snagging a beer, and taking a long drink. "Snoopy's only one dog."

"Remember, I bought an Alaskan Malamute at the end of the tour," I remind him. "Denali is in his kennel in our room."

"Snoopy loves other dogs." Eli tells me something I already know.

"Denali's a spirited puppy and a large breed; you sure Snoopy's up for that?" I ask, petting Snoopy in his arms. "The dog run is to the right of the pool. Once he does his business, he's welcome in the pool area."

"I'll take him out," Montana volunteers, arms already extended.

Eli's more than happy to hand over his pet to stay in the air conditioning with his ice-cold beer. Montana places a kiss on my cheek as she passes by.

"C'mon Snoopy," she babbles. "Wait until you see your potty spot. It's huge, and then, you can swim or sniff around all you want. Later, I'll introduce you to a new friend. His name is Denali. He's gonna be so happy to have a friend to run with him every day."

Eli's talking, but I don't hear a word. I tune my ears to Montana's baby-talking with Snoopy. *Could she be any sweeter?*

22

MONTANA

The Next Day

Peyton takes the afternoon off early to come join me at the pool. I introduce her to both dogs, and they entertain with much too much energy, sprinting around, hopping in the pool, and chasing each other.

The guys are in the studio, and I can't keep from glancing at its door behind our lounge chairs from time to time. Carson's showing the guys more lyrics he's written. He promised it wouldn't be long.

"So, how's married life?" Peyton says, noting my attention on the door behind us.

I smile at my best friend. She gave me the days I asked in L.A. to be with Carson without needing to call and report everything to her. I told her I needed alone time with Carson. Little did I know his parents would drop in and ruin that plan. I vowed to share everything with her upon our arrival in Des Moines, so the time has arrived.

"It's hard to put into words," I admit.

"Uh-huh," she shakes her head. "I'm not letting you off that easy. I want details." She sits upright and turns her body toward my chair.

"I promised I'd share," I remind her. "Just know my descriptions won't do it justice." I mock her position, turning to face her, my hands folded over my knees.

"So, we didn't get the alone time we'd hoped for," I begin my explanation. "When we pulled into his driveway, his parents were at his front door to greet us." I pause for her reaction.

"His mom gave the house manager the day off, they cared for the new puppy, and waited on Carson to get home. They claim they needed to chat with him before he went into seclusion for recording the new album, but they were there to meet me."

"And?" Peyton prompts. "Are they nice, or is his mother a raging witch?"

"She was nice enough. She interrogated me, but I held my own," I smile proudly. "After I answered her questions and assured her I wasn't in need of her son's millions, we had a nice 48 hours together."

"So, now tell me about you and Carson…"

"We've talked a lot. I told him about my parents, my brother, our lives in Iowa, and my indecision on my future." I take a sip of my iced tea and wipe the beads of sweat from my brow. "I love him. It's crazy; it's too soon, but I love him."

"Uh, duh," Peyton mocks. "I knew that on the night they married the two of you. Both of you are head over heels in love. That's the only reason I allowed you to elope."

Too bad she didn't make sure I wasn't blotto so I could remember it. I enjoy having the video, but actual memories of that ceremony would be better. I guess she had no actual way of knowing, though.

"We stay up late talking until we can't keep our eyes open any longer."

"Now, we're getting to the good stuff," Peyton cheers.

"Stop," I admonish. "We are taking it slow; we're dating. We've held hands, cuddled in a lounge chair on his rooftop patio while watching the waves at night, and kissed. Nothing more."

"Wait. What?" Peyton sputters. "You're married and newlyweds! You should be screwing like wild animals."

"Peyton, we consummated the marriage in Vegas, and neither of us remember it. We're trying to get to know each other. We didn't date, so we do that now," I explain. "And, you know me; I don't give it up right away."

"But you already gave it up right away," she reminds me.

"Be nice," I scold. "He's an excellent kisser."

"Good. Then, he'll be good in bed, too."

I swat at her. "That's my husband you're talking about. I don't want you thinking of him during sexy time."

"Oh. My. God. Please never refer to sex as sexy time," Peyton begs. "I think my ears are bleeding."

"Cannon ball!" Eli screams, running to jump into the pool.

How did I not hear the studio door open? I spin to find Jake and Carson approaching our lounge chairs. I rise to greet him with a kiss I've been attempting to stifle for over an hour.

"Get a room!" Eli hollers from the far end of the swimming pool.

"We have a room up there," I inform him.

"Well, use it. We don't need any of your marriage germs rubbing off on any of us," he declares, climbing from the pool, his red skinny jeans, t-shirt, and converse sopping wet.

"It's not contagious," I remind him.

"I'm going to put my suit on," he informs the group.

"Freeze," Carson yells, and Eli strikes a statue pose. "I'll bring your suit. You're dripping wet and shouldn't walk through the house like that."

"I'll come with you," Jake states.

I raise an eyebrow at Peyton. *Is Jake going to swim? No way.*

I assist Peyton in applying sunscreen to the backs of the three men. I start with Carson, and she starts with Jake. Eli comments that he's okay with sloppy seconds to which we shake our heads. As Peyton is taking her sweet time, ensuring Jake's safety from UV rays, I apply a thick coat of sunscreen to Eli's very pale back.

"Dude, you're gonna fry," Carson informs him.

"Sun screen will protect me. I'll just need to reapply it every hour."

He looks over his shoulder at me. "Will you set an alarm and make sure I do?"

I nod, hoping the others will assist me. It feels strange to be running my fingers over Eli's back.

"Spin," I instruct.

"No, I can get my chest." He snags the bottle of sunscreen from my right hand and heads to the patio table under the umbrella.

I turn my attention to Peyton; she's finally done fondling Jake in front of us. Now, the two are sitting at the edge of the pool, talking low enough we can't hear them.

We spend the afternoon floating on rafts, lazing at the pool's edge, and playing fetch with the two dogs in and out of the water.

"I'm headed to the cooler," Eli announces, using his arms to pull himself from the deep end, his back to us. "Who wants another?"

Jake, Peyton, and Carson all order another beer. When Eli turns, walking toward our end of the pool and the cooler, I gasp.

"Eli," I call to him. "Did you reapply sunscreen to your chest when I reapplied to your back?"

"Why?" he asks, looking down.

The guys laugh loudly at their band mate. Peyton laughs so hard she snorts.

I try not to giggle when I inform him, "You have two large, white handprints on your chest, and the rest of you is bright red. Let's go inside," I suggest. "The sooner we get aloe vera on you, the better you'll be."

Not helping, Jake and Carson cheer, "Atta boy," as he walks by. Eli awards them double middle fingers, grabs a towel, and follows me into the house.

23

MONTANA

In our bathroom, I pose Eli in front of the vanity mirror while I grab the aloe vera from my makeup bag. Thank goodness I took it to Las Vegas in case we spent a day at the pool.

"This will be cold," I warn.

"Then, rub your hands together," he urges.

I shake my head. "You want this to be cool to sooth your burned skin," I inform him. "We must reapply this often, like I did for you at the pool, not like you did." I can't help the giggle that escapes as I place my coated palms on his pectorals and spread the aloe all over his chest. When he squeals like a girl, I lose myself to laughter. "Atta boy!" I throw his favorite saying back at him.

Once I've slathered a thick layer over all of his screaming, red skin, I wash my hands then turn to face him.

"Can you do me a favor and record something for me?" he asks, opening his phone and extending it to me after I dry my hands.

He looks around the oversized bathroom and positions himself in front of the glass shower stall. "Start recording with only my face. Then, pan to include my chest when I mention it," he directs. When I nod, he begins, "Hello, all my Communicable Diseases. I'm posting today to share an interesting lesson I've learned. I've lived my entire life in California and traveled all over the world with the band. But after less than 24 hours in the Midwest, I've experienced my first sunburn."

He pauses, smiling as I zoom out to share his painful burn with the fans of the band. He places his palms on the white skin where he placed his sunscreen covered hands then removes them. "Evidently, sunscreen doesn't run or spread through osmosis. Lesson learned, my friends, and now, I'm paying the price." Looking up to the sky, he shouts, "Damn you Midwest sun!" Then, he signals for me to end the video.

"How'd it look?" he asks, snagging his phone from me to check it out.

"Love it," I tell him. "But I've never been fond of the band's followers being labeled the Communicable Diseases."

"Warner and marketing came up with that for our fan club," he informs me, something I already knew. "Aren't you a member of our fan club?" His expression of worry that I'm not as loyal to the band as he thought nearly rips my heart in half.

"I've been a proud fan club member since the club's inaugural year," I state.

"Um," he smirks, "so, you've been a Communicable Disease for many years now. Get used to it."

I shake my head. He's right, but it doesn't mean I have to like the title.

"What's the plan for the rest of the afternoon, like dinner?" he asks while carefully pulling a t-shirt over his head then chest.

"I need to run to my parents' house to grab more clothes, shoes, and stuff. I've been living out of the bag I packed for Las Vegas for over a week now."

"I'll ride with you," he excitedly offers. "I can't wait to see more of Iowa. Lord knows I don't need to spend more time at the pool."

"Okay," I respond. "Peyton will go with us. It shouldn't take but an hour, and we will be back in time for dinner with the guys."

Unraveled

Stepping back on the pool deck, Eli and I find Peyton's face tucked into Jake's neck and his hand on her ass as she sits on his lap. He's carrying on a conversation with Carson, distracted by her lips to his neck and ear.

"Peyton," I call, and she pulls her face from him to look in my direction. "I'm running to Mom's to grab stuff."

"I'm going with her," Eli informs the guys from the shade of the patio umbrella.

"Good," Peyton cheers. "Then, I'll stay here and soak up some more sun."

"The only thing in the sun is your feet," Eli informs her.

She sticks her tongue out at him.

I look to Carson to see if he has any interest in going to my parents' house and meeting Dad.

"I've got some fine tuning I need to work on." He rises, striding toward me. "I should be done in an hour; will you be back by dinner?"

His hands slide into my hair at my jawline, making it difficult to nod.

"Good, I'll get my stuff done and have the rest of the evening to spend with you," he murmurs less than an inch from my lips.

My eyes move from his eyes to his mouth, willing it to press to mine. He doesn't disappoint. A gentle kiss slowly simmers between us.

"Uh-hum," Eli interrupts sassily. "As I'm the only single male here, I'd like to mention that you both suck, and your public displays of affection are disgusting."

"Dude," Jake replies, "I'm still single."

Eli throws him a look. "I guess that's a tumor on your lap, rubbing your crotch and licking your neck, then."

"Easy," I sooth, pulling Eli from the shade into the house. "Carson and I will try to be more discrete."

As we walk through the house and hop into my white Jeep Cherokee, he explains, "No, you and Carson are newlyweds. You're supposed to be all over each other all the time. You need to be. I'm just having a weak moment. Maybe it's the pain of the sunburn making me bitchy."

I want to tease him about his low pain tolerance or offer to set him up but think better of it. He's flown from L.A. to Des Moines, he drank several beers, and he's now sunburned; I need not add to his long day.

When we enter my parents' home, Mom and Dad are both in the kitchen. She's pulling meat from the refrigerator for the grill, and Dad is fixing mixed drinks for the two of them.

"Well, hello," Mom greets. "To what do we owe this surprise visit?"

Before I can respond, Dad extends his hand to Eli. "Welcome. I'm Don," Dad greets. "It's nice to finally meet you."

"Um, Dad," I interrupt. "This is Eli Patrick, not Carson."

Embarrassed, Dad tries to cover. "The drummer, right?"

I glance to Mom then back to my dad; someone's been doing his homework. I make a mental note to ask Mom if she printed out information for Dad or if they researched online together.

"Yep, that's me," Eli smiles. "Carson's working in the studio, so I offered to ride with Montana. I'm eager to see more of Iowa."

"Welcome to our home," Dad extends a low-ball glass. "Would you like an Amaretto Sour?"

"Sure! I haven't had one of those in ages," Eli answers, taking the proffered glass.

"None for me; I'm driving," I remind Dad.

My statement causes him to smile. My parents like that I am careful with alcohol and motor vehicles. We've had more than one family friend in DUI accidents and have discussed it many times.

"Eli, wanna come see the rest of the house and help me in my room?" I ask.

He tells my parents, deadpan, before following my lead, "She just brought me for my muscles."

After a quick tour of the house, backyard, pool, and pool house, I pause before opening my bedroom door. "Now, what you are about to see is not, and I repeat, is *not* to get back to Carson."

Packing items to take with me is only half my mission. The other task is to remove all the band posters, record covers, trophies, and ribbons from my room before I bring my husband over to meet my dad.

"What have we here?" he teases, eyes wide, taking in my room.

"I've shared that I am a rock and metal fan," I defend. "I just haven't told Carson about the posters on my walls."

"Posters of sweaty, hot lead singers, bassists, guitarists, and drummers. All of which are not your husband, Carson." Eli sarcastically points out the obvious.

I swing my closet doors open, my hands and arms outstretched like a model, pointing out the Communicable poster.

"Poor Carson's heart will shatter if he finds out you hid him inside your closet, and it's a poster of the entire band, not just him. The other posters only have one guy in them and are on display 24/7."

I want to slap Eli. This is why I asked him not to tell Carson what he was about to see. I flop onto my bed with a deep sigh. Eli flops down at my side.

"Your secret is safe with me 'child bride,'" he vows.

"We need to come up with a new nickname for me," I remind him. I'm worried that the next one might be worse than the current one.

"Nickname can wait," Eli states, taking my hand in his as we lie on my bed. "You pack the stuff you need, and I'll handle the posters."

I turn my head to him, his already facing me. He nods his chin, pulls me with him from the bed, and pushes me towards the closet.

24

MONTANA

That night, after dinner, the guys invite Peyton and me to join them in the studio. Carson plans to unveil some lyrics, and they plan to create the music to accompany it.

I'm excited. I've seen bands on stage but haven't witnessed the creative process behind the songs. Well, other than watching *Songland* on TV. The way the three producers and the artists collaborate with the new songwriters mesmerizes me. I can't wait to witness it in person.

Peyton and I take seats on an over-sized chair in the studio while the guys each take control of their instruments. Carson and Jake sit with their guitar and bass in their laps. Carson moves a stool to him and spreads notebook paper full of lyrics in front of him while Eli takes the throne behind his drum kit.

They don't discuss a plan of action, and Carson doesn't read the lyrics to them first; he strums his guitar and reads from his pages. Jake plays a few chords now and then, and Eli watches.

I close my eyes, lost in the lyrics Carson sings. I don't catch every word, but what I hear touches me deeply.

"First to fall... doubt... not a guy believes in love at first sight... slap in the face, heart began to race... make me a believer..."

It's the lyrics he wrote after we bumped into each other in the

Unraveled

hallway and went out as a group that first night. He's writing about his reaction to me. My heart swells as tears well in my eyes.

"Wow," Peyton whispers, turning to face me. "You may have a hard time telling me how you feel about him, but he definitely has no trouble describing it."

I nod, smile, and wipe the tears from my eyes before they can fall to my cheeks.

"I can't believe my best friend has a rock song written about her," Peyton giggles.

I'm silent; I can't speak. The love and emotions swirling inside of me are too much. Carson plans to share these lyrics with the world. The world will know exactly how he feels about me. It's heady, it's sweet, and it's so much more than I can ever give to him.

I'm lost in my own thoughts for so long that when I become alert in the studio again, the guys are experimenting with lyrics to another song.

"Risk... must..., gifted... not a tryst... dust... Play my part... trust... hair mussed... heart... lust... I was lost... box... come undone, unravel me."

The words "unravel me" repeat many times in the chorus; that should be the title of this song. *Unravel Me*. Carson unraveled me; according to these lyrics, I've done the same to him.

"Face front... don't look back... celebrate the end of loneliness... the end of bachelorhood... no longer solo or a lone wolf."

I'm hot from head to toe, my skin prickles, and my heart thumps in my ears. I stare at Carson—my man, my husband. Every part of me longs to jump on his lap, wrap my arms and legs around him, and rub against every part of him. I need him; I want him. Every part of him, inside and out, calls to every part of me.

Peyton rises from our chair, stretching her arms above her head and yawning for all to see. Taking his cue, Jake returns his bass to its stand before following her to the door.

I look to my phone; it's past nine. Peyton is not ready to head home. Instead, she's going to Jake's room. My desire for Carson grows stronger each day. I find the need to make love to him consuming more and more of my thoughts and time. Remembering my conversation with Eli earlier about making out in public, although I want to take Carson up to our room for the rest of the night, I won't.

Late the next afternoon, I'm sitting at the edge of the pool, fighting tears, and watching the dogs in the backyard.

Eli emerges from the house, sneaking up behind me in his stealthy way. "How's Snoopy? Is he behaving?"

I startle, nearly falling forward into the pool. I quickly attempt to settle myself. I nod while wiping my cheeks discreetly. "You know that Snoopy was a beagle, and not a Jack Russell, right?"

"Thanks; the band let me know that right away," Eli shares, taking a seat beside me. "He looks more like Snoopy with his coloring than most beagles with their brown and black patches."

"Why are you out here, not in the studio with the guys?" I ask, not liking silence with him so near.

"I need fresh air to clear my mind; it helps with creativity," he states.

I nod.

"What's with the tears?" he asks, bumping his shoulder into mine.

"It's nothing," I lie.

"Nothing doesn't cause tears; it's something."

I shake my head.

"C'mon! I'm a superb listener," Eli urges.

"It's..." I let out a huff of air. "I need to get my act together." I pause, lifting my long hair off the nape of my neck in one hand, resembling a ponytail. "This house is full of people working, working toward something, and I seem to tread water."

"I get that," he states. "But you have a job, and you are working. You're a newlywed, and you're working on your marriage. That's a job, especially with a rock band in tow."

I shrug, "Not an actual job. There's so much we don't know about each other. It's like we are dating now since we didn't before."

Unraveled

"I see the way the two of you look at each other. You're crazy in love. You're good for him. He's been lost for too long," Eli shares.

"It's crazy; it doesn't seem real," I admit.

"If you don't need to work, enjoy some time to relax." He taps my temple. "Your next decision between college or job will come to you when you're ready," Eli promises.

"I don't feel like a grownup. I'm supposed to be wise and responsible."

"If you mention that to your parents, I bet they tell you adulthood is a lot of faking it," he says, kicking his bare feet in the water. "Heck, when I'm not behind a drum kit, I do not understand what I'm doing. I don't date, I can't make friends—the band is my family. Sometimes, I think I'm fine right where I am, but all too often, I daydream about more."

"You deserve more," I state, hoping he realizes it.

"That's easier said than done. We can't all bump into the love of our life in a hotel hallway." He bumps against my shoulder again.

"Well, the first step is being open to the possibility. Now, tell me what type of woman we are looking for," I pry.

"We?" he counters.

I nod.

"Not high maintenance, easygoing, fun, and hot. She has to be hot. Do you have a sister or cousin like you?" he asks, only half teasing.

"Ah, that's sweet. I think it'll take someone more interesting to keep your attention." I bump his shoulder back.

"Drop it," Eli instructs. "I need to focus on the album."

That night, Peyton and I find a moment alone in the kitchen, fetching snacks. "What's it like being married to the famous Carson Cavanaugh?" Peyton asks. "It's hard to believe you're a wife now."

"I'm bored all the time. Denali, Snoopy, and I spend too much time together," I groan.

"So, do what you planned to do this summer, before you went and got married. You had summer plans," she reminds me.

"Well, I planned to hang out with you," I smile sweetly at her.

"Duh," she teases.

"And, to do some career and school research," I remind her. We spoke about it before our trip to Las Vegas.

"So, do that," she states as if it is just that simple.

"I guess I could work a bit at Mom's office, too. I've tried to stay at the house, because I'm worried about the paparazzi swarming me like they did in Las Vegas and L. A.," I confess.

"It's Iowa—you're safe," Peyton argues.

"I think I'll wait until Warner arrives before I plan days out and about."

"Okay," she draws out.

"You'll still come visit me all the time, right?" I ask.

"Or at least until Carson tells me I can't be here. I mean, you have a pool. You must force me to stay away," she chuckles.

"Maybe the reason I'm so wishy-washy on my next step is because God planned for me to meet him," I suggest.

"So, you've met him," she counters. "Now, it's time to do your research, find what makes you happy, and spend some time on your future, too."

"Maybe I'll work with our Bra-Claw idea for a while until I'm ready to do something else," I state.

"That's a fabulous idea," Peyton agrees. "You loved working on your app, then marketing, and finally selling it. I know I came up with the Bra-Claw idea, but you brought it to fruition. I'll help when I can."

"Then, it's settled. For now, I'll be an entrepreneur," I smile at my best friend. "Let's take the dogs for a walk before they're put in kennels for the night," I suggest, seeking more time with her.

"How do I seduce my husband?" I ask when we're safely outside the house.

Peyton guffaws and stops abruptly which jerks Snoopy to a halt.

I continue walking. "I mean, should I just tell him? Or is it better if I hint at it?" I query further, looking directly at my friend, desperately seeking her advice.

"You're serious?" Peyton asks. "Okay, well, what have you done in the past with guys to give them the green light?"

My jaw drops in disbelief. She knows I'm inexperienced with men. I'm not the leader in my relationships. *How did I think I could do this?*

"Hey." She waves her hands in front of my face to get my attention. "So, you've shared that you cuddle at night while talking. That's a perfect time to drop your hints. Every touch can be a signal. Brush against him; place your hand on his arm, his chest, and his jaw."

She leans closer to me. "Dress provocatively, forget a towel when you shower and holler for him to bring you one, or walk naked in front of him as much as possible."

"I don't know," I hedge. "What if he ignores me?"

"You make it impossible for him to ignore you. He's a guy; he won't need over one or two hints," she explains, taking my hand in hers. "I think he's struggling with the whole 'taking it slow' plan. He's a good guy, so he's giving you the time he thinks you want." She squeezes my hand, smiling. "Trust me, he's ready."

I swallow hard and nod. Maybe she's right. Heaven knows she's way more experienced than I am. I'm not keen on flaunting my naked body, but I could hint a little as we chat in bed. I nod. *I can do this; I'm ready.*

Carson

While the girls walk the dogs, I waste no time squirting a dab of shower gel in my hand. I lather up my hand as I allow the spray to cover my chest and flow southward. I've used up all of my restraint for the day; I'm desperate.

I glide one fist down my shaft followed by the other. The slick soap allows my motions to glide smoothly up then down. I place my left palm on the tile wall, under the showerhead. With thoughts of Montana's tight body on my mind, I imagine what she might look like naked, showering with me. I tighten my grip and quicken my strokes.

Although I'm sure it will pale compared to the real thing, I fantasize my fist is her hot, wet heat, clenching around my shaft. On its own, my pelvis thrusts into my palm, once, twice. Fire shoots from my center as I spew my seed onto the tile near the shower floor. My body shutters, and a low groan echoes in the shower enclosure.

The warm water pelts my back. I close my eyes tight, and I lean my forehead on the cool blue tiles. I can't believe I'm resigned to my second shower of the day. I need to find another way to channel my desire for Montana. I can only take so many showers in a day before my housemates figure out what I'm really doing in here.

We met days ago, yet it feels like we've been together much longer. After eloping, I thought it best if we took a few weeks to get to know each other better before I initiated sex. I spend my day sporting a boner at the sight of her, at the thought of her. It's barely been a week, and the blue balls are nearly killing me.

Perhaps I should slowly start laying the groundwork. I can kiss her more, hold her more, and cuddle with her in bed at night. It will be torture as my body will only desire her that much more, but I don't want to rush her. I rushed her into marriage; I can't rush her into sex. I need her to trust me and come to me when she's ready. I just pray it's sooner rather than later.

25

CARSON

I'm in the kitchen when Warner's driver buzzes in at the front gate. I shoot a text to Eli and Jake, alerting them of his arrival.

"Did you see where Montana went?" I ask.

Fran nods, pointing to the front room. When I walk through the doorway, I find Eli, Peyton, and Montana in a tight huddle. They are planning something. Jake descends the stairs, a giant smile upon his face. Jake rarely smiles and never this wide. The hair on the back of my neck stands on end; something is up, and I don't like it.

Eli pulls the two wooden doors open, and we step onto the front porch to greet Warner. Off to the left, I notice a large truck and matching trailer with "Randall Farm" printed on the side, sitting at the edge of the driveway with a large black and white cow tied to the back of it. Now, I know what the gang was whispering and giggling about.

We move back inside and out of the way for Warner and his entourage. Three young men assist a label rep in caring several crates of liquor and boxes of food into the foyer. Warner doesn't grab his bags; instead, he waltzes in with a blonde woman under each arm and a sleazy smirk upon his face.

"Atta boy," Eli champions Warner's choice in travel companions, slapping him on the back.

Warner's heavy footfalls echo in the large foyer as he escorts his women to the living room sofa. The girls giggle at his sides. I roll my eyes, and Montana elbows me in the ribs.

Warner goes to check out his bedroom, not taking bags with him. "What the fuck!" he yells before a door slams, and we hear his boots clomping toward the top of the stairs.

"Real fucking funny," he announces, leaning his arms on the railing. He looks down to the group. "Ha, ha, ha, you got me," he deadpans. "Thanks for the cow in my room. I'd blame it on Eli, but the truck out front has Montana's name all over it." He turns to look at her from his perch. "You're officially part of the family now, and it's open game on pranks."

Montana nods, smiling. "I know you are concerned about leaving L.A. women for the cows in Iowa, so I arranged a welcome party for you. Call it Midwest hospitality."

"Thanks for putting me in my place; now, escort the cow out of my room then sanitize everything before you carry my bags up."

Montana scoffs loudly. "Um," she climbs the stairs, "I'll lead the calf from your room, but the room's already clean. Your bags are your own problem."

I love that she's comfortable enough with the band that she gives as good as she gets. Leading the calf slowly down one stair at a time, she speaks to it. "You're much too good for the likes of Warner. I should have brought a mule for him. That's the closest thing we have to an ass. And, don't let anything he said bother you; he's used to blonde, twiggy bimbos climbing all over him. My grandma would call them hussies. You're much too good for him; never forget that."

Montana pulls the calf through the front door. At the sight of its mother, it bawls.

"Dude," Eli looks to Warner. "I think it's a male."

The group laughs.

"Perfect," Warner whines. "Now, she thinks I'm…"

"No, I don't," Montana interrupts, returning. "And, it wasn't a male. I know the difference."

"Carson," Warner says, "you've got a real winner here. If we're ever stranded, she'll know how to help us survive."

Montana

After listening to Warner grumble for hours about missing his life in L.A., I pull Peyton aside. The two of us plan to show the guys fun in Des Moines tonight.

Warner and Jake motion for Peyton to join them on the sofa. I quirk an eyebrow in Carson's direction. He smirks back at me. *What is going on?* He waggles his eyebrows at me. Maybe it's best I don't know what he knows.

"What's up?" Eli asks.

"We're taking you out tonight," Peyton answers. "We're gonna show you fun--Iowa style."

"No thanks," Warner says. "I'd rather stay in and wash my hair."

"Too bad," Peyton retorts directly to his face. "I wanna go out, so we're going out. And you, mister, will have fun."

Warner rolls his eyes in our direction.

"How long until dinner is done?" Peyton asks.

"An hour," I answer.

"Okay, upstairs, all of you," she orders. "We need to help you fit in. We don't want the entire city to recognize you on your first night in town."

"What's wrong with the way we're dressed?" Warner asks.

"Just trust us," Peyton pleads.

"So, this is the Brickhouse," I inform the group as we walk the three blocks to the little corner bar. "Tonight's open mic night. There will be a couple of bands performing in thirty-minute sets. Then, a local band will perform sets the rest of the night. Sometimes, they do covers, sometimes only their songs."

"Great," Warner drawls out. "High schooler-wanna-be-rockers are my fav."

Peyton swats his arm. "You promised."

"And, so did you," he reminds her, referring to an agreement the two made in private.

I reach for the door handle, but Carson quickly pulls it open for me. He's such a gentleman. I pause inside until all of our group enters. I point to two open bar stools at the corner of the bar. Peyton and I hop onto the stools while the four men surround us. A band scurries around the small stage, preparing for their session.

Carson

A tequila shot down and beers in our hands, we visit in the tiny, yet noisy, bar. A high-pitched sound of feedback proceeds the announcement, "And now, Blue Biscuit."

The crowd applauds, and the band starts right in with a cover of Buckcherry's *Crazy Bitch*. The band is good instrumentally, but their voices aren't great. At the end of the song, the guitarist apologizes, claiming their lead singer couldn't make it tonight.

"Put us out of our misery, Carson," Warner shouts over the noise. "Go be their lead singer."

I shake my head. "Let them work it out."

"Our next band's running late, so order drinks. Our headliner, DnD, will take the stage at 10," the manager announces to the crowd while Blue Biscuit tears down their equipment.

"Have we heard DnD?" Peyton asks.

Montana smiles wide, nodding. "They're the Dungeons and Dragons band."

"I want to leave by 10 then," Peyton tells the guys.

"Should we?" Eli asks, lifting his chin towards the stage.

"You think the kids would loan us their gear?" Jake asks, his face excited.

I approach the manager, now back behind the bar. "Hey, mind if we fill in for the absent band?"

His brow furrows, and he states, "I knew you guys looked familiar. Have you played here before?"

I shake my head, fighting my smile. He motions for me to take the stage, so I approach the bassist at his case.

"Dude, would it be possible for us to borrow your instruments for a bit?" I ask. "We'll buy your drinks while we perform."

The kid rises, quickly tilting and turning his head to toss his long bangs from his eyes.

"Fuck!" he shouts. "You're..."

"Yes, can we use your instruments?"

"Yeah, man. Of course." He rambles, waving his bandmates over. They put their heads together, and I can't make out what he tells them. When they part, all four are star struck and speechless. I wave for my bandmates to join me then slip a fifty-dollar bill from my wallet.

"For drinks," I state loudly near his ear.

I approach the mic stand. "Hey, if you don't mind, my friends and I wanna play for you. Let's give a big round of applause to the Blue Biscuits for loaning us their stuff."

A few members of the crowd clap while others look on judgingly.

"Who the hell are you?" a man near the back yells, and several audience members nod, also wanting to know.

"Let's just say you'll recognize us in a moment. We are bored and hopped over to Des Moines for a while."

The crowd cheers approving of us in their city, even if they don't recognize us.

Each of us play a few notes, getting the feel for the strange instruments. The crowd boos, thinking we don't know how to play. Pissed at the crowd's response, Eli bangs out a four count, leading us into our first number one hit. Just like that, the crowd figures out our identity and goes wild.

For the next 30 minutes, we play through our catalog in chronological order. The crowd grows larger by the minute. By the time we're done, police are at the door, and the fire marshal's pushing customers out the door. I'm sure someone posted on social media, causing word to spread like wildfire.

We didn't keep the fact that we're recording our album in Iowa a secret. We don't plan to hide, but we might consider security on our next outing.

Blue Biscuit greets us as we exit the tiny stage, handing each instrument back to its owner. Always ready, Eli produces a black permanent marker for us to autograph the instruments.

We slowly push our way through the crowd, back to our girls. It's clear we can't stay here. I call the manager over and ask for his help with the police to slip us out a backdoor. I have to give it to the Iowa fans. They are not as intrusive as they are in other cities. They don't follow us to the back or swarm our car as we drive away. It's a pleasant change of pace.

26

MONTANA

The Next Morning

I take my laptop down with me to breakfast. The guys are still sleeping as they worked past three last night. They'll rise about noon, eat lunch, then return to the studio; it's their new daily schedule. Peyton and Mom both work every weekday, so I plan to chat with Fran for a while before I take Denali and Snoopy to the dog park or walk on a trail.

I nibble on my breakfast as I bring my laptop to life. "What's on your to do list today?" I ask between bites.

"I'm making a grocery trip about ten-thirty, I'm fixing burgers and fries for lunch, then there's laundry and cleaning to be done upstairs in the afternoon," Fran shares. "What are your plans?"

I shrug. "None really. Walk the dogs or go to the dog park. Maybe swim in the backyard or read while I get some sun." I'm embarrassed I have nothing important to do. I don't want people to think I'm freeloading off of the band. "I've already started laundry for the guys."

"Montana," Fran chides, "it's my job, not yours."

"I know, but I have too much free time." I tell her something she already knows. "I don't mind. It's only two loads twice a week.

Anyway, I'm used to doing my laundry, washing dishes, cooking, and cleaning. It's hard to let someone else do it for me." Fran gives me a stern look with hands on her hips, but I see her smile break through.

"I want to make a treat for the guys; could I add a few items to your grocery list?" I feel bad for asking; I have more than enough time to run to the grocery store myself.

"What are you making?"

"Scotcharoos," I explain. "They take five ingredients and are easy to make. I'll make two batches. Trust me, they are so good; two batches will not be enough."

"I've never had them," Fran confesses.

"If you have 10 minutes this afternoon, I'll show you how to make them." I try not to sound too eager. I know Fran has work to do. I probably bother her too much. I really need to find something to busy myself.

I busy myself caring for the dogs and visiting Fran while she works. At PetSmart, I introduce Denali to the clerks and sign us up for a training class. I purchase too many toys and chews. It's easy to get carried away; there are so many fun things to play with.

After lunch, I hold both leashes as we walk toward the lake. Denali and Snoopy love the water; so, I throw a tennis ball from the dock, and they dive in to fetch it over and over. When my arm grows tired, we return to the house.

Tomorrow, Denali, Snoopy, and I plan to join Mom for lunch then play at the dog park on her side of town. She loves dogs, and it gets the three of us out of the house for a bit. I feel I spend more time with them than I do Carson. I don't see Carson except for his 30-minute lunch breaks or on the nights they emerge from the studio before midnight.

Eager to see my man, I interrupt the studio session by taking them my Scotcharoos. I realize their work is important, but I can't help myself. I'm in desperate need of human attention.

I quietly make my way down the hall, slowly opening and closing the door to the booth where everyone watches through the glass while Warner sings.

Eli hops from his chair, sniffing the treats I hold. "Break time," he yells, forcing Warner to stop his vocals abruptly.

"What do we have here?" Carson asks, then places a kiss at my temple.

"I made Scotcharoos," I tell them. "Trust me, they are to die for."

As if on cue, Eli elicits a moan of pleasure while he chews.

"That good, huh?" Carson asks.

I bite my lips and nod.

Warner relieves me of the tray. "You bake, child bride?"

"I can bake," I answer, not bragging that I am a superb cook. It's a detail I need to share with my husband before the entire band.

"Holy shit," Jake mumbles with his mouth full.

Carson nods in agreement as he chews.

I lean near his ear. "I made another batch just for the two of us. I'll hide them in our room."

I love the twinkle in his eyes. I guess it's true what they say. The way to a man's heart is through his stomach.

I catch myself ogling him every chance I get. *How weird is that?* We're married, and I feel guilty for lusting after him. It's only been two weeks; essentially, we've only dated two weeks, and I'm revved up like a brazen hussy.

My mind drifts to fun fantasies and sinful scenarios. My hands itch to grip his ass and pull him towards me. I crave his hard body pressed tight to mine. Even my dreams involve sex with Carson. The more we're together, the more I get to know him, the more I long to connect with him in every way. *I wonder if he feels the same...*

27

MONTANA

Two Weeks Later

Peyton and I spend the afternoon poolside with margaritas, currently we are on our second pitcher, delivered by Fran. After floating in the pool on mats, now we lounge under the patio umbrella as we dry off and plan to shower then change before dinner.

The guys emerge from the studio.

"Explain to me why we spend hours in the studio when we could be out here, enjoying the gorgeous view?" Eli asks the guys.

"While I agree the view is gorgeous, I'd advise you to keep your eyes on Peyton and off my wife," Carson warns.

Eli throws his hands up, stepping towards Peyton's lounger. An indescribable noise rumbles from Jake, causing Eli to excuse himself and head into the house.

"Don't move," Warner orders in our direction. "We'll grab our suits and meet you back out here."

I pretend I don't see his eyes waggle suggestively to Peyton as I try not to giggle.

Seems the lead singer is smitten with my bff. The bad boy of rockn-roll seems to have lost his desire for a wide variety of ladies. Though he won't admit it, he's lost his desire to go out and plunder in Des Moines. He's happy to hang at the house with Peyton.

Minutes after Carson, Jake, and Warner head into change, Eli emerges from the house, his arms carrying a cooler with beer which is busting out of the top.

"Thirsty?" I tease.

"We're celebrating," he informs.

"Celebrating what?" Peyton sits up, moving her sunglasses atop her head.

"We officially have two songs done for the album," Eli boasts, popping the top off his bottle of beer.

"Cool." Peyton grabs a beer from the cooler while I still sip my last margarita.

Carson

"Last beer," Jake states, opening his bottle.

"I guess we must move the party inside," Peyton offers, always up for keeping the fun flowing.

"Can I hear the songs you finished?" Montana attempts to whisper, slurring her words.

I chuckle, rise, and offer my hand to my wife. She sways a bit on her feet, so I pull her tight to my side.

Warner chuckles, "She's a lightweight." He points at Montana.

"No, she's not," Peyton swats his chest from her perch upon his lap. "The two of us polished off two--, count them-- two pitchers of margaritas before we switched to beer with you. And, Fran has a heavy pour."

Montana then comes to her own defense. "We started drinking at noon today." She stares at her phone then asks me, "How many hours ago was that?"

Of course, everyone hears her.

"C'mon. Let's go listen to the tracks," I urge.

The others follow our lead.

I love watching her reactions. Although she's read my lyrics, now with the music and all of the band's voices, my words come to life.

Montana

"I'm bored," Eli whines. "Let's play a game."

A game? Did famous drummer Eli Patrick just suggest we play a game?

He opens the fridge, passing beverages to everyone.

"We're playing two truths and a lie," Eli states. "Montana, you go first."

I nod. *I can do this.* Two truths and a lie. "I'm a certified skydiver. I'm allergic to chocolate. I've sold an app I created for millions of dollars."

"Carson and I have to sit this one out as we know the answer," Peyton offers.

"Well, now, this is interesting," Warner croons. "If I had to guess immediately, I'd say allergic to chocolate is the most boring of the three. It has to be true."

Wow. This guy doesn't have a filter.

"She's smart," Jake states his opinion. "I could see her creating and selling an app."

"With Peyton as her best friend, I wouldn't put skydiving past her," Eli adds. "Hmm, I say the lie is she's allergic to chocolate. I didn't see her eat a Scotcharoo, but I doubt she'd make them if she's allergic to them."

"I'm not a certified sky-diver," I share. "I am allergic to chocolate. It's not deadly. I break out in hives for 24 hours."

"Eli and Warner, drink up," Peyton taunts, and they quickly down their entire drink and grab another.

"Let's make this more interesting," Warner urges. "Let's play truth or dare instead."

Four sets of eyes look to Peyton and me to see if we will play.

"I'll go first," Eli announces. "I dare Peyton to kiss Montana."

"Really?" Peyton asks. "You go straight to that one with no warm-ups?"

"If you don't feel comfortable, you can always choose truth," Carson offers.

"We don't mind," Peyton informs. "It's not like it's the first time."

The guys look on with wide eyes and open mouths. We share a kiss halfway between sisterly and porn stars, and they don't hide how much they enjoy watching.

Peyton asks Eli, "Truth or dare?" She makes a point to show that he did it wrong last time.

Eli chooses truth, and Peyton asks if he's ever taken part in a three-way.

"Nope," he answers. "I've never been lucky enough to get an invitation."

He turns his attention back to me. "Montana, truth or dare?"

As much as I want to take the easy way out by choosing truth, I need to choose dare and impress the guys. "Dare."

"Give Carson a lap dance right here." He points to the chair Carson currently occupies.

"I'll need music," I inform the group.

Walking toward my husband, *Closer* by Nine Inch Nails fills the room, and I begin.

I've never given a lap dance before or witnessed one at a strip club. I have watched several shows containing them, so I harness my inner goddess and begin. I sway my hips slowly from side to side then forward and back, side to side and forward and back again. I bend at the waist, keeping my legs straight, and slap the floor between my feet. I look to Carson between my legs. Slowly, I slide my hands up my legs as I return to a standing position.

I spin around in time with the music, placing first my right knee in the chair beside his thigh, then my left. My hands on the back of the chair at either side of his head. I grind my happy place against the fly of his jeans. A small breath of air escapes my lips at the sensation of his rock-hard cock where I desire it most.

Instantly, the rest of the room fades away; he's the only one here with me. I repeat the movement of my hips over and over, the song setting my pace. Carson's hand settles on my hips; his fingertips dig deliciously into my flesh. My breathing picks up, and Carson's nostrils flare.

"Uh, hello? The song's over," Peyton's voice breaks our spell.

My eyes widen with the realization that I just gave the band fodder for future spank-bank material. I feel my cheeks heat as I crawl from Carson's lap.

His hand flies out, grasping my wrist, pulling me to his lap.

"Don't wiggle," he growls into my ear, his hot breath prickling the skin of my neck.

The group sits silent for a moment before Eli reminds me it's my turn to choose someone.

"Carson, truth or dare?" I toss over my shoulder.

"Truth."

"Rate that lap dance on a scale of one to ten compared to the others you've had," I order.

Without a thought, he answers, "Ten. The best I've ever had." He kisses my shoulder.

I want to ask how many lap dances he's had in his lifetime, but I'll save it for our private pillow talks.

Carson chooses Warner who picks truth, much to my surprise. When asked if he's in a monogamous relationship, Warner answers no but that he wouldn't be opposed to it.

Hmm. That's interesting. Seems my husband's as curious about the three of them as I am.

"I choose Eli," Warner announces proudly. "And, you can't choose truth."

"Dare," Eli says.

"I dare you to show Montana *all* of your piercings." Warner's proud of himself.

My eyes dart to Carson, unsure what's about to occur. From what I know of Warner, I can only assume one of Eli's piercings is below the waist.

Eli approaches where I sit on Carson's lap. "You can't punch me for this," he tells Carson while unbuckling his belt. He lowers his pants to reveal his erect and pierced cock.

I don't dare count how many piercings he's adorned his genitalia with. It's not polite to stare, but how can I not? He's a mere five feet away from me, exposed and proud.

"If you get your cock pierced, there will be *no* blowjobs," I inform my husband, my index finger pointed in Carson's direction.

"D-A-M-N!" Warner draws out.

Suddenly, I realize Carson might already be pierced, and I don't remember from our drunken wedding night.

Carson spins me on his lap, crushing his strong lips to mine. His kiss is a powerful and demanding one. I follow his lead, open my mouth, and express my desire for him as he doesn't hide his need for me.

We're all lips, tongues, and hands exploring. Moments pass before I come up for air to find the studio is empty. We are alone. The others slipped out without us noticing. I don't give them more than a second's thought and return 100 percent of my attention to my man.

While my lips rejoin his, my hands unfasten his belt and unbutton his jeans. I slip my right hand down, palm to his abdomen, until my fingers reach the target. A hiss escapes him when I grasp his heavy, rock-hard cock fully in my hand. I'm startled when his hand grabs my wrist, pausing my movements.

"Are you sure you are ready?" he asks, his voice gravely. "I mean, we've been drinking…"

"I've been ready for a while," I interrupt him. "I'm very aware of exactly what I'm doing. Now, hush, and let me get to know my husband intimately."

He releases my wrist, and I resume my exploration, stroking him. My left hand unzips his jeans, and taking my cue, he shimmies his jeans and boxer briefs low on his hips, offering me unfettered access to him.

Part of me wants to back up and take him in; a bigger part of me seeks an intimate connection, so I continue my strokes, adding a second hand. Carson's head relaxes on the back of the chair, heavy-lidded eyes peering at me.

I wiggle myself from his lap, still caressing his heavy weight in my hands. My knees on the carpet, my eyes on his, I part my lips, daring my tongue out to touch the tip of him. Wanting more, I slide my tongue in a circle around his tip. Still wanting more, I lower my mouth, taking him in inch by inch.

Eyes still on his through my lashes, I slowly slide farther and farther down his shaft. When his tip taps the back of my throat, I swallow, allowing my throat muscles to tighten around him.

Carson snarls, pulls me from my knees, crushing his mouth to mine. On their own, my hands remove his shirt as he tears off mine. Breathing heavily, we stare at each other for a moment before removing our remaining clothes ourselves.

Naked, we stand a foot apart, chests heaving. I extend one hand, placing it over his heart; its rhythm is as fast as mine. When I lick my lower lip, it stirs Carson back to action. He pulls me tight against his hard chest. His hands grasp my backside, lifting me. I wrap my legs tight around his waist. My breasts smash against his strong pectorals, and one of his fingers traces my hot, wet folds.

"Yes," he growls, positioning his tip at my opening. Then, eyes on mine, he thrusts into me.

Carson

Nestled within her, my heart swells, and my world's complete. I'm hers, and she's mine; we're finally together in every way.

Montana's so tight, wet, and warm; I need to calm myself. I've waited for this; I've fantasized of this. I don't want to lose control too soon. I need to make her feel good first.

Impatient, Montana wiggles her hips. I remove my mouth from

hers and smile. She knows what she wants, what she needs, and I'm the luckiest man alive because I'm the one that will deliver.

I back up one step then another. My heel meets the bottom of the chair. I release her ass with my right hand, place it on the arm of the chair, then lower us to sit. When I scoot back in the seat, Montana positions her knees at either side of my hips. I grasp her hips, pulling them forward.

"Oh... god... yes!" she moans, sliding her hips forward and back while grinding herself on the forward strokes.

With her hands over my shoulders, her fingertips bite into my skin. I slide one hand between us, seeking the button to catapult her, to rocket her over the edge. My fingers part her swollen lips, and I place the pad of my thumb on her swollen bud, making tiny circular movements.

"Yes! Yes! Don't stop!" she screams at my contact. "Please! Please..." A feminine growl escapes her throat as I keep the pace. "Y-e-s!"

She grinds herself tightly to my pelvis; her nails pierce my shoulders, and her inner walls, with vice-like strength, grip my shaft. Wave after wave her muscles contract, milking everything from me.

Her forehead falls upon my shoulder while we come back to earth and attempt to slow our racing hearts and rapid breaths.

"I'm glad," I gulp in a breath, "that this studio is soundproof," I tease.

"What?" She lifts her head. "Were we loud?"

"Well, one of us was," I state.

I'm not sure if she's blushing or her cheeks are pink from our physical activity. Her eyes are bright, and her lips are swollen. Sex looks good on her.

"We should dress," Montana offers, slipping her arms into her bra and refastening it. I remain seated as she shimmies her lace panties then her shorts up her long legs and over her hips. I continue taking in her body until she slides her shirt back over her abdomen. "Everyone will know what we've been up to."

"They left knowing," I explain.

She tilts her head and bites her lower lip as she watches me redress.

"Like what you see, Mrs. Cavanaugh?" I tease.

"Umm," her eyes find mine. "I guess it'll do."

Giggling, she runs from the studio. I grab my shoes then dart after her. She's already out the exterior studio door and across the patio, entering the house.

"You better run," I holler after her. "Just wait until I get my hands on you."

I can hear her laughter when I enter the house. I nearly catch her on the stairs.

"What's all the racket?" Eli asks, peeking his head into the hallway from his bedroom.

At his words, Montana pauses at our bedroom door. I don't acknowledge him. Instead, I throw her over my shoulder like a fireman.

"Carson!" she squeals, out of breath and laughing.

I step into our bedroom, nudging the door shut with my foot. In three long strides, we're next to the bed, and I throw her. The wrought iron headboard bangs loudly against the wall, and the bed frame squeaks.

She props herself up on an elbow to watch me slowly and stealthily lock the door. When I slide my t-shirt up then over my head, she licks her lips, her eyes locked on my abs.

Stuck in a trance, she lifts her fingers to caress my stomach muscles as I near. Her touch feels like feathers; her fingertips swipe over each bump and hard plane. I suck in a ragged breath as she lightly scrapes her fingernails on the same path.

My eyes lock on her liquid brown ones as she continues to bite her lower lip. She dips her index finger in the waistband of my jeans, her pouty lips forming an "O" when she contacts my still-hard cock.

Montana

. . .

Unraveled

His nostrils flare as I run my finger along his shaft; then, he pounces. He drags me up to the head of the bed, his mouth entertaining mine while his hands divest me of my halter top and shorts.

My flesh prickles against the cold air. The sensation energizes my desire. Cason pulls his lips from mine to gaze down my body. I squirm under his view. He licks his lips, eyes on my mouth as he sits up, knees planted on either side of my hips. I glide my hands up his sides and over his ribs in an attempt to grasp his neck and lower his mouth back to mine. My arms aren't long enough, and Carson smirks, realizing what I want and withholding it from me.

"Please," I whimper, breathy.

His tongue emerges from his parted lips to lazily swipe his lower lip, the lower lip I want to nip and suck. My body is afire with fevered need. Every part of me needs to feel every inch of him, skin to skin, mouth to mouth, and limbs wrapped tight.

Aching to hold him, I wrap my twitching fingers around the metal bars of the headboard. The cold, smooth metal grounds me for the moment. Carson stares at my hands, gripping the headboard. He falls to his elbows, inches above me.

"Don't move," he growls. His right hand covers both of mine, gripping tightly. "If you let go, I'll stop."

I search his face; he's not kidding. My man likes the thought of my hands handcuffed or tied above my head. I can appease him; it'll be fun. The rough pads of his fingertips skim down my arm and over my shoulder. I fight a shiver while biting my lower lip. I'm pinned beneath him, at his mercy and hot with all the possibilities. I've never trusted a partner as I do him. I've never given over all of my power and allowed a guy to pleasure me. Somehow, I've trusted him from the moment we met in Las Vegas.

28

CARSON

We're making great progress in the studio today. So far, Eli and Warner aren't bumping heads, and we're recording great tracks. Warner's singing the last verse of what may just be our first single on this new album. Jake and I man the sound board while Eli shares directions with all of us. He's proving to be a talented producer.

"Shit!" Warner blurts.

Well, we were making significant progress.

Eli flips the mic switch, "What's up?"

"My cell phone won't stop buzzing." Warner pulls it from his back pocket. "It's Meredith; let's take a 10 minute break."

Jake and I groan in frustration as we hoped to lay this entire track down today. I look to the clock. It's nearly six p.m.

"Might as well make it a supper break," I inform the group, rising from my chair. Before leaving, I look back to Warner, still in the studio. His back turns towards me, and his hand rubs the back of his neck.

I pull my cell from my pocket, turning it back on. Some of us actually follow the rules and turn our phones off to limit distractions while we work. Moments pass before three missed texts from Meredith ping. I read them in order.

> **MEREDITH**
> call me NOW!
> urgent issue CALL ME!
> NEED 2 SPEAK 2 U & WARNER!!!!

I delete them as Warner's on the phone with her now. Eli and Jake have left; I hang around to hear what Warner has to say. It turns out to be several minutes before he ends his call.

"Fuck!" Warner screams, throws his phone against the padded studio wall, and kicks over two music stands.

I exhale before opening the door. "That bad?" I query.

"She's pregnant," he states, facing me, his hands in his hair.

Gone is the always confident trouble-maker. Before me stands a broken man. I might even say a scared man.

"Sit," I instruct, motioning to the large chair behind him. "Give me the details."

He falls into the leather chair, letting out a long, loud breath.

"Remember last fall? Our four concerts on the east coast?" Warner doesn't look to me or wait for me to answer. "There was a woman at all four venues. Security let her through backstage and to the tour bus. I messed around with her once, but I wore a condom. My own condom. There's no way the baby's mine."

"The timeline fits for her to be eight months by now." I tell him what he doesn't want to hear.

"I wasn't the only guy she fucked. I fucked her once; God only knows who she fucked at the other three concerts where she earned her way backstage," he spits. "She claims it's mine; she's looking for the biggest fish to get her payday."

While I don't like his slut-shaming the woman, groupies allow many types of men to enjoy certain favors to gain the access they seek. I've heard security and roadies brag about blowjobs and sex from women desperate to get to the band.

"We need to talk to the guys and then to the crew to see if they remember her at the venues. If their stories match yours, you may be able to keep her from going to the press." My friend doesn't seem eased by my words. "What will you do if the baby *is* yours?"

"It's. Not. My. Fucking. Kid," he bites. "She'll get nothing from me."

Warner storms from the studio, slamming the outside door. I tap my phone to call Meredith. I need all the details to handle this for our band. I text the guys, too.

ME
band mtg 30 min

Warner remains in his room during our meeting. It's better this way; his inability to fathom that it might be his child doesn't help us get ahead of the media.

"Shouldn't Montana be here?" Eli asks when I try to start our meeting.

"Yes; she's part of us now," Jake agrees.

"Montana," Eli yells from the kitchen.

Soon, she peeks her head in.

"Have a seat," I urge, eager to get this over with. "Meredith has been contacted by a lawyer representing a woman claiming to be eight months pregnant with Warner's baby." I pause, giving this heavy news a chance to settle.

"Dude, how many times has this happened already?" Eli says. "Eventually, the women admit they aren't pregnant or refuse to take part in a paternity test."

"This woman is eight months pregnant, the baby bump is real, and she's requesting Warner submit his DNA for the paternity test." I repeat what I learned from Meredith.

"Damn..." Jake's shaking his head in disbelief. "So, who is she?"

"Meredith didn't give me her name, only that she attended our four east coast concerts last fall, was given backstage and bus access at each one, and states she had sex with Warner," I share, watching Montana to gauge her reaction.

"I remember her," Eli announces too loud. "Not her name, but I remember I couldn't believe she was a regular person, not a celeb, and made her way back at all four venues. That never happens."

I look to Eli as he speaks, corroborating part of her claims.

"I saw her and Warner leave the green room together," Eli continues.

Jake enters the discussion. "Warner always wears a condom, and it's not one someone gives him. He carries his own at *all* times."

I'm surprised when Montana jumps in on the conversation.

"Condoms are only 98 percent effective at preventing a pregnancy," she informs. "That's when they're used perfectly every time. New studies show the average man applies his condom correctly only 85 percent of the time." She looks to me and shrugs.

"Fuck," Eli reacts, throwing his hands in the air. "How come they don't tell us guys that? I mean, a guy should know there's up to a 15 percent chance the condom will fail. I deserve to know that." He doesn't hide his frustration.

"The condom box warns that they are 98 percent effective when used properly," Montana states. "The other information is in several magazines and available online."

"Who reads the back of a condom box?" Eli scoffs. "Do you?" He points to me. "Have you?" He points to Jake. We both shake our heads.

"It's his baby, isn't it?" Eli surmises, plopping back into his seat, defeated.

"Not necessarily," Jake states. "If she hooked up with someone at all four concerts, there may be other men on the hook for this one." He faces Eli. "You saw her all four times? Where was she? Was she with any guys?"

"Not that I remember," Eli confesses.

"Try to remember," Jake orders, desperate to prove Warner innocent.

"So far, she's agreed not to go to the press," I explain. "Meredith's arranging a meeting near us for Warner to meet with the woman and her attorney. Unless his DNA isn't a match, I'm afraid Warner will need to step up and take responsibility."

"This sucks!" Jake says what we are all thinking.

"Warner's refusing to do the paternity test, claiming there's no way he's the father," I share. "The easiest remedy is for him to agree to the DNA swab."

"I'll talk to him," Jake promises.

Montana

I feel like I'm right in the middle of an entertainment show publicity scandal. Like Jake said, "This sucks!" I understand the woman's need to seek the father of her unborn baby. On the other hand, though, I can't imagine Warner's fear that he might be the father. I suspect he fears the DNA result, and that's the reason he's protesting it so.

I try, but my mind can't help but wonder how many women Carson slept with while on tour. Having witnessed the women throw themselves at the guys while in Las Vegas, I'm not sure Carson could have refused many of them.

I refuse to sit here and wonder about this all night. I snag a bottle of vodka from the bar and head toward Warner's room. I knock lightly three times.

"Leave me alone," Warner snarls.

I ignore his demand, turn the knob, and find it's unlocked. I slip inside, shutting it behind me.

"I come bearing a gift," I state, extending the vodka bottle for him.

"Thanks," he bites, his chin motioning for me to head back through the door and leave him alone.

I join him, sitting on the floor, leaning against the foot of the bed.

"I don't want to talk about it," he states before chugging from the vodka bottle.

"Okay," I agree.

We sit quietly for several long minutes. I take a long pull from the bottle when Warner offers it to me.

"Carson didn't mess around," he declares, nudging my shoulder with his. "Not with groupies or a girlfriend."

I let his words sit for a minute.

"We teased him about it," he chuckles. "I do not understand how he does it. He can go forever without sex. It's unhealthy how long he deprives himself."

I like Warner's words. I hope he's being honest with me. I mull it over for a while.

"Are you, Peyton, and Jake in a thruple?" I blurt the question which has been bothering me for weeks now.

"Thruple?" he parrots in question.

"You know, a threesome?" I reword my question.

Warner laughs at me, a deep belly laugh. "A thruple?" he slurs his words a bit.

"It's a real word. I've read about them," I defend. "It's a combination of threesome and couple."

"You've read about them?" he inquires.

"Yes; I read all the time," I explain. "Occasionally, I enjoy a steamy romance, and that's where I've learned all about them." I change directions. "I see the way you react to Peyton."

"I…"

I'm not sure if he's stuttering or slurring.

"Don't deny it," I argue. "I know she excites you. And, my best friend seems to reciprocate those feelings." I glance sideways at this face in the pale light from a YouTube video paused on his iPad on the floor beside him.

"She's important to me, and I don't want to see her hurt," I continue. "So, are you in a relationship or not?"

He takes a long pull from the bottle before stating, "We're adults. If she wants you to know, she'll tell you. Otherwise, keep your nose out of it."

It becomes harder to understand the more he slurs.

"If you hurt her…"

"What?" he taunts. "You'll what? Cut off my balls? Tarnish my image in the press? Tell Carson to punch me?" He chuckles, shaking his head.

I try a different approach. "Have you ever been in love?"

To my shock, he answers, "Yes," his voice low.

"What happened?" I continue, hoping to learn more.

"She was the sister of my roommate and bandmate." He plays with the now empty vodka bottle in his hands. "She's the reason I looked for a new band all those years ago."

I remain silent, although I want to pry. I feel lucky he's opened up to share so much already.

"I messed around with another girl outside a bar during intermission. I was drunk, but that's not an excuse."

Again, we are quiet for several long moments.

"Do you think I deserve this?" he asks into the darkness.

I shake my head. "No one deserves this. But you need to find out one way or the other."

"I can't be a father," he states, defeated.

"I don't agree," I admit. "You have options, you know. You could offer money if you are the father. You could be involved in the child's life. The days of forcing a man to marry the pregnant woman are far gone. Before you decide how involved you want to be, you need to find out if the baby's yours."

Warner remains quiet beside me.

"I believe you'd make a great father. I've seen glimpses into your paternal side with the guys and with fans," I share. "A baby would be lucky to have you as its father and in its life."

"Were you a virgin when you married Carson?" he slurs. "You seemed so sweet and innocent..." His head bobbles on his shoulders.

"Let's get you into bed," I suggest, tugging his arm.

"Carson won't like you in bed with me," he smirks.

Perhaps drunk Warner will open up.

"Do you like Peyton?" When he nods, I continue. "Are you in a monogamous relationship with her?"

"Nope," he answers, popping his 'p' and upsetting me. "I share... trup... thrup..."

"Are you in a thruple?"

Unraveled

He nods.

"Are you sleeping with other women?" I dig deeper, needing to know.

"Only Peyton..." he mumbles.

There; I have what I wanted. Warner cares for her.

Warner continues slurring words I can barely make out. Worried he took pills, I scan the room. I'm relieved to spot an empty liquor bottle rolled under the foot of the bed. He's drunk and out like a light. He's too heavy for me to lift into his bed. Instead, I place a pillow under his head and toss a blanket over him.

29

MONTANA

A Week Later

I pat the pillow next to mine before I open my eyes. Carson's already up, and we left the curtains open. It's much too bright in here. I raise my hand to shield some of the late-June sunlight. Hearing the shower, I look towards the bedroom door. Denali isn't there; I guess he already took our boy out this morning.

I stretch my arms over my head, breathing deep. *How is it I just woke from a full night's sleep and I'm still exhausted?* My muscles feel heavy. Perhaps breakfast will give me energy to wake up.

I snag a hair tie from my bedside table, securing a high ponytail as I descend the stairs. A big yawn hits me at the bottom step, and I place my hand over my mouth as I cross the front room. I'm wiping the corners of my watering eyes when I enter the kitchen.

Carson

Fresh from my shower, I towel dry my hair then secure the towel around my waist. I smile at my reflection; I can't wait to wake Montana and reveal my plans for us today.

A female scream tears through the house. I lean into our bedroom; she's gone. *It's Montana!* I sprint from our room and down the stairs, hopping from the third step to the tile floor below.

I narrowly miss falling from water dripping off of me on the marble of the front room. I use a Scooby-Doo-like maneuver until I gain traction and run into the kitchen.

I'm unable to speak or catch my breath when I stand in the doorway, finding Montana wrapped in another man's arms as Fran and another woman watch.

She pulls away, wiping tears from her eyes. "What are you doing here? And, why didn't you call me? I could've picked you up at the airport." Before the man can respond, she asks, "How did you get here?"

"Mom brought me over," he admits.

As if on cue, Montana's mom appears beside me.

"Carson, aren't you a little under-dressed for breakfast?" Tony teases, pointing to my towel.

"Carson," Montana acknowledges my presence, "why aren't you dressed?"

I run my hand over my stubbled jaw. "I didn't have time when I heard your blood-curdling scream."

"Oops," she giggles, covering her mouth. "It surprised me to see my brother, that's all."

"Your brother," I repeat. "Nice to meet you. I'm Carson."

"Oops," Montana giggles again. "Joe, this is Carson. Carson, this is my big brother, Joe."

"So," Joe lifts his chin towards me, "he's not the usual rock star, huh?"

He's pointing out my nudity. Montana swats his shoulder.

"Be nice," Tony Randall orders her son, complete with a mom stare.

"Oh my gosh," Montana gasps, drawing my attention back to her.

"You must think I'm incredibly rude. In my excitement, I didn't notice you," she explains to the familiar woman sitting at the breakfast bar. "Wow, even that sounds rude. You're much too pretty not to be noticed. I'm so sorry," she rambles and extends her hand. "I'm his sister, Montana. I saw you playing guitar during our last FaceTime call."

"I'm Starr."

That's why she looks familiar.

"And this is my husband, Carson," Montana introduces. "But I'm sure you've heard Joe rant all about him."

Starr smiles her mega-watt smile. "I might recall him mentioning something about a wedding," she teases. "And, Carson and I've already met."

I find the confused look on Montana's face adorable. I should let her gnaw on Starr's statement for a bit as payback for taking years off my life when she screamed. But I won't.

"Starr and I met at the MTV Video Music Awards a couple of years ago," I inform the group. "Now, if you'll excuse me, I should get dressed."

Montana

I'm so excited to see my brother that I barely entertain the idea of following my man upstairs and ripping the towel from his waist.

"Why didn't you tell me Joe was coming back for a visit?" I ask Mom.

She doesn't answer, simply points to my brother. I turn to face him, waiting for an answer.

"I wanted to surprise you for your birthday, silly," Joe confesses, playfully punching my forearm.

"This is the best birthday gift *ever*!" I announce, hugging him again.

"Did someone say 'birthday'?" Carson asks, back in the doorway, still wearing only a towel.

"Didn't she tell you?" Joe smirks. "Tomorrow's her birthday."

Carson

I want to wipe the smirk from his face. He's purposefully making everyone aware I don't know my wife's birthday. But I won't hit him. He's her big brother, and he's concerned for her; I'm glad he is. Also, if I punch him, my towel would probably fall, and that's not what I want to share with my new family.

I smile at my wife, and she smiles back. I nod my head, while inside, I'm frantically searching for an idea for her gift.

Montana

Carson excuses himself for the second time, and I aim my attention back to my brother. His hair is much longer and messier than he usually styles it. I like it. He looks softer, more relaxed. He's always been too serious and very focused on his career. Before me stands a new version of Joe.

"I'm afraid to ask..." I cringe at my shaky voice. "How long can you stay?" I scrunch my nose, bracing for his response. I can't wait for it. "Please, please, please stay in the U.S. I mean, Iowa. Please stay in Iowa. I need you here, near me," I plead. "A girl needs her big brother. Don't go back to Africa."

Joe pulls me to his chest, wrapping me in a tight hug. He kisses the top of my head before responding, "I might be able to arrange it."

My breath catches while I replay his words to ensure I didn't misunderstand.

"You'll probably be bored of me in a week," Joe teases.

I don't find it funny. "You'll really consider staying?" I ask hopefully.

Starr slaps him on the back. "Stop teasing her and tell her already."

I blink my eyes several times as if that will help me understand.

"I'm home to stay," he states slowly.

"Now, *that's* the best birthday gift ever!" I announce, and the kitchen fills with laughter.

"You mind keeping it down in here? You've got the dogs all riled up," Eli says as he opens the patio door.

Denali and Snoopy rush past him, straight to me. We've spent so much time together, they're anxious to see that I'm alright. I'm sure my scream earlier worried them. I bend down to pet them. Denali's heavy paws at my shoulders push me flat on the floor. I laugh as the two dogs nuzzle and lick my cheeks, chin, and neck. You gotta love the way dogs share their love.

30

MONTANA

"You know, many couples get a dog to prepare themselves to become parents," Carson's mother tells my mom.

I'm lounging in the sun in the chair next to theirs. My eyes are closed, and they believe I'm asleep. Wanting to hear what they say next, I keep pretending.

"A grand baby may be in our future." My mom claps excitedly.

"They rushed into marriage," Carson's mom reminds mine. "It would be okay if they took their time in starting a family."

"Do you have any grandchildren?" Mom inquires.

"No; do you?"

"No. I can't wait. I do look forward to it," Mom states. "I assumed my son would give me my first grandchild, but he doesn't stay in the U.S. long enough to meet a girl. Although, I don't know what to make of Starr traveling from Africa with him."

"She knew the band; maybe she tagged along to see them," Carson's mom offers. "I've got another son and a daughter, both married, but they plan to wait until in their 30s to start a family. They have too many things they want to accomplish first."

"Did you plan all of your children?" Mom asks.

"No. Did you?"

"Heck no," Mom answers. "Maybe God will gift us grandkids sooner rather than later." Both giggle; then, I hear them tap their glasses together.

My queasy stomach beckons for a snack. I find Starr placing snacks on her paper plate, too.

"I'm still on Africa's time," she explains. "Usually takes a good four days for me to settle when I return."

My plate full of snacks, I pause to talk. "Do you fly from Africa to the States often?"

She nods, chewing her last bit of food. "I try to visit Africa once or twice each year. It's hard to squeeze it into my busy tour and recording schedule."

"I apologize." I place my finger over my lips as I swallow a bite of cracker. "I'm not familiar with your work." I meant to search for her online last night, but Carson had other plans for my hands. I smile at the delicious memory.

"No worries. I'm not exactly mainstream," Starr explains, swirling the ice cubes in her drink. "I'm known in Jazz and Folk circles."

I nod. I'll need to research her and listen. I enjoyed the music in mine and Peyton's Jazz dance classes. I'm sure I'll enjoy hers.

"I collaborate in other genres; that's how I know the guys," she chuckles. "I can't believe they have a connection to Joe. Yesterday was a surprise for me as well."

"I enjoyed watching you play your guitar with the children in the village," I say then take another small bite of cracker.

"The children are my favorite part of my visits," she states, fiddling with her phone. "I also enjoy the photos I take." She extends her phone to me. "Scroll," she directs.

Her phone in hand, I marvel at the photos of the African scenery, the people, and even Joe, who she's caught providing medical attention to the communities. I swipe slowly, enjoying each photo of a land I hope someday to visit.

Unraveled

The next photo includes Starr and Joe. They stand side-by-side, their joined hands between them. There's an elderly man with his hands up in front of them as the community surrounds them. It looks like a ceremony of some sort. I search the photo for more clues.

"What's this?" I question, tilting the phone for Starr to see which photo I'm on.

Her eyebrows rise high on her forehead, and her lips from an "O." Instantly, I know she didn't mean to share this photo.

"Um…" She takes back her phone, scanning the pool area for my brother. "I guess…" She returns her gaze to me. "It's supposed to be our little secret," she states. "Follow me."

I grab two more crackers before following her into my parents' house. She doesn't stop in the kitchen as I expect; instead, she leads me out into the garage, shutting the door behind us.

"Okay," she starts. "Joe hasn't told your parents yet, so you have to keep it a secret." I nod, and she continues, "The tribal chief performed a marriage ceremony for us on our last night in the village."

My head tilts to the side, and a smile slowly spreads upon my face. That little devil. He lectured me about my eloping in Las Vegas, yet he does the same thing in Africa. Wait until I get him alone, I'll--

"We plan to tell your parents." Starr interrupts my thoughts. "Joe's waiting for the right time."

"Trust me, there is no *right* time," I chuckle. "So, the two of you are married?"

Starr nods, a gorgeous smile on her face and twinkles in her eyes. "I spent a month in the region last year, and we grew close. This year, I've visited twice and…"

I wave my hand in the air. "No judgement here," I promise. "I'm so happy for you and thankful you brought him back to the U.S. I've really missed him."

She can't stop smiling; she's positively beaming. "Our marriage isn't legal in the States; eventually, we'll need to make it legal."

I nod, unable to speak. I'm ecstatic. Already, I see that she softens him, getting him to relax and enjoy life. The fact that he's not headed back to Africa in a few days is even sweeter. It seems everything in my life is falling into place.

31

MONTANA

When we return to the backyard, I pull on my swimsuit coverup. I find that Carson and Eli man the grill full of burgers and chicken breasts.

I join my brother near the kitchen door, placing all the fixings on the long table. Working as a team, we position the buns, condiments, onions, tomatoes, lettuce, chips, and dips. Mom and Dad set up a cooler of water, beer, and pop.

Taking turns, we fix our plates soon after then scatter around the patio and poolside, gathering around tables and chairs. Sporadic conversations continue while we enjoy dinner. Dad commends Carson on the burgers and asks which seasoning he used. The two discuss the best flavors of seasonings and barbecue sauces. Luckily for me, the band is on their best behavior, and we enjoy hours with my family.

"Time for gifts," Mom announces.

Carson takes my hand and leads me to the round table by my parents. He pulls out a chair for me, kissing my exposed neck before sitting himself. A pile of perfectly wrapped boxes appears in front of me. Peyton unloads two paper bags. Apparently, they plotted to hide the gifts so I wouldn't protest.

I scan the group of family and friends gathered to celebrate my twenty-first birthday while my father lights the candles on my birthday cake. This is my new family; it's grown this year, and I'm blessed that it did.

"Hold up," Eli orders before the crowd sings the birthday song. "It says 21. You're already 21."

"Um…" Peyton smirks at me by my side.

"Nope; she turns 21 today," Mom answers.

"But you…" Eli continues his attempt to understand.

"Did you tell them you were 21?" Dad asks.

I shake my head. "It never came up," I explain. It's the truth. "I never got carded in Las Vegas."

Mom bites her lip, shaking her head at my actions. It's no surprise to my parents. They know Peyton and I drink. They've lectured us on safe drinking and not driving.

"So, you really are a child bride," Eli states, proud of the nickname he labeled me with.

"Can she blow out her candles now so she can open my present?" Peyton pleads.

I'm curious to find out what she bought for me. "I'll blow out the candles, but you're not singing to me," I announce.

They argue with me a bit, but I get my way. Of course, Peyton ensures her gift's on top of the pile on the table in front of me. I take my time, ripping the beer-can decorated paper, and I pull a frame from the box. It's two five-by-seven, golden-brown frames connected with hinges. I pull them open to find my wedding vows on the left and Carson's vows on the right. This simple gift of our typed vows inside a frame means the world to me. She approves of the words, our marriage, and wants me to see our vows every day.

Tears well in my eyes, and I fan my heated face.

"What is it?" Mom asks.

I pass the frames to her then turn to face Carson. He wipes my tears with his thumbs and kisses my cheek.

"I love you," he murmurs.

"I love you, too," I return.

"I didn't mean to make you cry," Peyton promises.

"I know." I've almost recovered from my tearful moment.

"These are the vows you recited at your wedding?" Mom queries, her brow pinched.

I nod, realizing she's not seen my wedding video that Eli recorded. I find the words we shared in our inebriated state perfect. It's clear she only reads the ramblings of drunks.

"I've got the video," Eli offers. "I can share it with you."

He's only trying to help, but I fear my parents won't find us responsible, level-headed adults, pledging our lives to each other. I want their approval, but I've grown to love our Las Vegas Wedding Chapel nuptials.

"Next gift," Joe prompts, trying to help me move on from the awkward situation.

I select the smallest box on the table, carefully pulling the ribbon and wrapping from it. Suddenly, I realize there is no card, and there's no "to" or "from" on it. I pause, the lid in my hand, almost revealing the gift inside. "Who's this from?" I ask my family.

"It's mine," Carson confesses beside me. "I suck at gifts. Guess I forgot to get a card." He shrugs, smiling his sexy, quirky grin.

Excitement bubbles within me at the possibility of the small, three-by-three-inch box. I bite my lower lip as I slowly slip the lid from its base to reveal a shiny, silver key on red, crimped papers. I take the key into my hand then toss it from one hand to the other.

"The key to your heart?" I look at my husband for confirmation.

He shakes his head. "The key to our house," he corrects. "It's much more than that, really. It's the key to all of me, to everything I have. You have all of me."

"Shew-wee!" Mom fans her face with both of her hands, tears in her eyes.

I smile, and my belly warms at my mom's reaction to Carson's gifts and words.

"He's a songwriter, that's for sure," Joe states, complimenting Carson on his choice of words.

I continue opening more gifts. The final one is from my parents. It's an eight-by-eleven-inch box, decorated in royal blue wrap with a Carolina blue ribbon, my favorite colors. Under the lid, I find a deed. I pick it up, scanning the details amongst the legal jargon. Mom shakes the bottom of the box, drawing my attention to a key. I pick it up, holding it on top of the deed. I see an address. Needing more details, I look to my parents.

"We purchased a small building for yours and Peyton's business." Mom smiles proudly.

Peyton joins me, reading over my shoulder.

"There's an office, a storefront of sorts, and a nice-sized warehouse behind it," Dad shares. "As you've created your second business venture, we thought it was time for you to set up shop for all of your enterprises."

"Thanks," Peyton says before I get my chance.

"Thank you," I respond, rising to hug each of them. "You shouldn't have. I have more than enough…"

"We know," Mom stops me. "We want to help you girls get started. It's an investment in the two of you and in real estate, so it's a win-win."

Part of me worries it's a way to keep me in Iowa and not in L.A. with my husband. I chide myself for such a thought. I'll save it for later; for now, I plan to celebrate.

"Seems keys were a theme," Eli teases, hugging me. "Wish I'd known. I would have bought you a car."

"Stop it." I swat at him. "I like the vintage tee more than I would a new vehicle."

"Even a vintage Mustang?" he teases.

"Well…" I tease back.

32

MONTANA

Later that week

We're sipping iced tea by the pool, my foot in the water, and Peyton is tanning, topless, on a nearby lounge chair.

"So, last night…" I begin the conversation I've longed to with my best friend.

"Finally!" She sits upright, not covering her bare chest. "Tell me everything. Leave nothing out."

"Cover yourself first," I prompt.

Peyton joins me at the pool's edge.

"Peyton, are you happy?" I ask.

Peyton crinkles her brow. "I thought you were going to tell me all about you and Carson. You want to know if I'm happy?"

"I mean with the… uh… guys." I worry my bottom lip.

Peyton smiles wickedly. "I thought you didn't want details."

"I don't," I quickly state. "I worry about you being happy and safe. I mean, you've never spent two weeks with the same guy before."

"I'm not with one guy; I'm with two," she corrects.

"Have you discussed what you want from your... uh... relationship?" I pry.

"Yes, Mom," she teases. "We've agreed it's just the three of us until one of us informs the others they want out. So, don't worry; we're monogamous."

"And, they take good care of you?" I continue. "Do they treat you with respect?"

Peyton smiles lovingly. "They take *excellent care* of me." She waggles her eyebrows.

"That's all I need to know." I quickly end that topic of conversation.

"Now, let's talk about you and Carson," she prompts.

It's Wednesday of the next week, and I've a billion things to do. Carson's already in the studio when I wake. I forego a shower, grab a quick bite, then lock myself in the office. I reached out to Carson's father last night, hoping to get some ideas on marketing our product. We're set to meet in a videoconference on Monday.

I swallow my last bite of cherry toaster pastry as I enter the office. What a mess. I take in the piles of papers I've spread out on the floor. Today, I need to focus on a presentation for Carson's father, explaining our product so he can best help me with a marketing strategy. The piles on the floor will need to wait.

I settle myself in the large, leather office chair behind the desk. I move a stack of papers, freeing up room to open my laptop. While I wait for my presentation software to open, I check my cell phone calendar for today through Monday.

Crap! I have a doctor's appointment this afternoon. Although it will be a quick visit, I call the office to cancel, promising to call in later this week to reschedule. I just can't deal with that today.

I settle in, creating a presentation complete with videos, online and in-person sales figures, and demographics. I'm nearly finished with the rough draft when there's a rap at the office door.

"Yes?" I call.

Fran appears in the doorway. "When you didn't break for lunch, I thought I'd better interrupt."

She places a tray on the two large stacks occupying the corner of the desk. In its center, there's a paper plate with a sandwich and chips. Next to the plate is a glass of ice, a bottle of diet cola, and two bottles of water. Everything practically fills the tray.

"Thank you, Fran." I didn't realize I'd worked five hours since breakfast.

She quietly exits, closing the door behind her.

I continue working while I eat; I need to finish the first draft of the presentation today and gather items to print for my meeting with Kurt.

Mom wants to meet Peyton and me at our new location in the morning. I'd reschedule, but I've already done that once. Hopefully, it will only take an hour, so I can get back here to work.

I've got a conference call with a potential manufacturer in the afternoon and another with the company supplying our packaging the next morning. I need to gather our current fees and information along with sales projections to complete those conference calls.

It's a good thing the band works all day until late at night. I need the hours to get organized and prepare myself for meetings.

33

MONTANA

Monday

I greet Kurt and Aaron at the door with uncomfortable hugs. They are still new to me, more like strangers rather than my new in-laws. Fran notified me mere minutes ago that they were at the gate. We'd planned a video call for today; I had no idea they'd fly to Des Moines. The guys are recording in the studio, so I won't let Carson know they're here until after our marketing discussion.

Fran and I offer our new guests a snack and drink before I invite both into the office. Aaron settles in the large, leather armchair by the library wall. I encourage her to share her opinions on the product, marketing, etc. as she'll be one of our key demographics. I begin by showing the product, our current packaging, and the examples on the dress forms with and without the product. I explain our attempts at naming and slogans: "Bra Claw," "a-BRA-cada-BRA," and "Now you see it; now you don't."

When I finish my presentation, I'm met with silence. It's silent for too long. I grow hot; I'm nervous they don't find our product worthy of his marketing. Aaron smiles, but like her husband, also remains silent. I begin to freak out. Silence can't be good. *Crap! This is bad. My in-laws don't like our product! This will throw a wrench in our newborn relationship.*

"Wow," Kurt finally gives feedback. "You have a solid platform for us to add to." He smiles wide.

I think he's proud of me. Perhaps I'm proving to Carson's parents I'm not seeking his money and fame.

"My turn," Kurt states, and he hands me a manilla folder.

I slowly open the cover, finding an outline with three major categories.

"I suggest we focus on these three avenues of marketing," he informs, pointing at the outline. "My team threw together this plan of attack, and we're ready to assist with each."

I'm stunned. He didn't just come here to hear my ideas and lend me a hand; he planned ahead and even brought his team in to assist us. My eyes blink rapidly, hoping to fend off my tears.

"As you see here, we plan to create banners and pictures for you to use on all social media platforms. We've contacted our two hottest influencers with ties to the Midwest. Both are on board, eager to receive the product and start promoting."

While he continues to explain, I hear not another word. One of the influencers is Peyton and my idol. She's the Olympic Gold Medal Gymnast that trained at our gym when we were in our first years of gymnastics. *Peyton's gonna lose her shit! Forget Peyton—I'm losing mine.* She's agreed to promote our product. We'll be working together. I need to sit down before my legs buckle. Both Peyton and I follow her on social media, we often discuss the products she promotes, and now, she'll be promoting for us. *No. Freaking. Way.*

"So," Kurt's voice calls me from my errant thoughts, "what do you think?"

I can't admit I didn't pay attention, so I smile and nod. I'm sure my eyes gleam. There's no way I'm concealing my excitement.

"I love it," I manage to reply. "I can't believe you put all of this together so quickly. I figured I'd pick your brain during our call."

I close the folder, clutching it tightly to my chest. "How much do I owe you?"

Kurt looks to his wife before he looks to me, smiling. "Pro Bono for family."

I shake my head. "I have the funds--"

He interrupts. "Consider it our wedding gift for our new daughter-in-law."

Tears fill my eyes; I press my lips together and nod. As much as I want to argue, I can't. I asked for his help, he's already done the legwork, and he can't undo it. Besides, I really, really want to work with the two influencers he has access to.

"Thank you," my weak voice trembles. "I can't tell you how much this means to me, to us. Peyton and I never expected this much help. We'll be forever grateful." I pat the manilla folder I hug tightly.

"We're happy to help," Aaron states, rising from her chair. "Based on the research we've conducted, I think your product will be a hit. I, for one, can't wait to try it." She stands before me with hands on my shoulders. "Now, let's go interrupt the boys and surprise my son." She slides her elbow around mine and walks me from the office.

When his parents come into view through the large, glass window, separating the production area from the recording studio, shock and worry flood Carson's face.

"What's wrong?" he asks through the studio mic, filling the booth.

I open the door to the studio. "Nothing's wrong. I asked your dad to help me with some marketing—I didn't plan to mess with your recording schedule. I'm sorry."

He shakes his head, smiling. "It's okay. A break will be good for the four of us. We've spent too many hours in this little space without windows to the outside world."

I wrap my arms around his neck, looking up at him through my lashes. "I love you," I whisper.

"I know," he teases, guiding me into the booth. "Let's break for the day."

"I'll be at the pool," Eli announces.

"Remember sunscreen," I tease him. "Set an alarm on your phone."

"Yes, child bride," he sing-songs.

I hear Jake murmur to Warner, "I'm texting her now."

I still worry about Peyton getting hurt in their little threesome arrangement, but she swears she's got it all under control. There's no way it's as casual as she claims. I hope, when the album's done, the three can still get along for Carson's and my sake. They really seem into my friend.

34

MONTANA

Weeks Later

After Carson's parents' visit, Eli announces he's been working on a special project that he is ready to share with us. I'm seated on Carson's lap as he sits on the sofa with Jake and Warner. Eli flips a few buttons on the soundboard then plays his work.

Music fills the small room from speakers in the ceiling and walls. The band loves his production, asking to hear it again. I can't put my finger on it, but there's something different about this piece; it strays from their usual recordings. I listen closer the second time he plays the track.

"Hold up," Warner directs. "Increase the volume on the second moan."

Eli fiddles with the soundboard and replays the section twice until they agree it's better.

All blood drains from my face, and my jaw drops. I point at Eli as I rise from Carson's lap. "You and I need to talk. Now." I push Eli's shoulders toward the music studio.

Carson follows us.

"In private," I inform, shutting the door before he enters the room.

"Ooo..." The other band members sing and laugh.

I motion for them to head back to the house. When it seems they've all left, I round to face Eli again. "How could you?" I spit.

Eli fanes confusion.

"You plan to exploit a private moment," I bite, spittle flying from my mouth with my words. "I thought we were friends." I wrap my hands around the back of my neck. "Were you spying? Did you watch us? Is that your thing?" I'm appalled.

Palms out toward me, Eli explains, "I only flipped a switch to start the recording; then, I left."

"Why me? Why us?"

"No one will ever know," he promises, tracing a finger in a cross pattern near his heart.

"But I know," I state. "You can't expect me to let you use it for the entire world to hear."

Behind me, the door opens. Carson joins us. "What's going on?"

"Your buddy, Eli," I share, "he... Those breathy sounds, those moans... That's me. That's us having sex. Eli recorded us." There, I said it. Now, Carson will handle the rest.

My husband's face isn't as angry as I expected. Instead, he smirks proudly.

"Seriously? You're okay with every man in the world hearing me, even jacking off to my sounds?"

He doesn't respond. We stare at each other, the rage inside me dying to explode, to escape, while he smiles back at me. I lick my lip before biting on it. Carson's nostrils flare, and his eyes lock upon my mouth. I stare at him for several long moments; the anger inside me wanes with each passing second.

Carson's gorgeous looks, sexy smirk, and memories of his actions that elicited those sounds from me wash away my desire to kill Eli for doing this to me, to us.

"You're really okay with this?" I ask my husband. He takes my hands, pulling me flush against him.

My head pressed to his chest, he whispers. "I didn't know it was you. And, if I didn't recognize it, no one else will."

I look up through my lashes. His warm brown eyes comfort me. I nod, letting out a long breath. My mouth quirks to the side.

"Okay." I turn to face Eli on the other side of the room. He's lying sideways in the oversized chair without a care in the world. "I'm sorry if I over-reacted. I've been so tired lately." I try to excuse my tirade. "I'm not happy you recorded me without my permission and planned to use the tape. In fact," I look to Carson for his support, "now that you've dubbed the sounds you want, you'll give us the recording. I'm not okay with you having it around." A chill shivers through me. "And no one, and I mean no one, better ever find out that's me you used for the song. You're lucky I'm so vested in those lyrics, or I'd tear your arms off for exploiting my first time with my husband. Without arms, I wouldn't have to worry you were jacking off to the recording."

"Um... second time," Eli corrects.

"What?" I'm lost.

"It's actually the second time you've been with Carson." He smiles sheepishly, still lying in the chair.

I make a move to attack, but Carson wraps both arms around my waist, pulling me back into him.

"I can't believe you want to argue with me when I apologize and give you permission..." I struggle against Carson's hold, attempting to attack his friend.

"Go," Carson orders, and Eli quickly complies. "And, don't record us again," he yells after his friend.

35

MONTANA

The Next Morning

I wake deliciously exhausted from our session in the studio followed by hours of lovemaking here in our bed. I take my time stretching my arms over my head then pointing and flexing my toes. Beside me, Denali groans as he stretches, too. He takes up more of the bed with each passing week; he's going to be huge.

My phone informs me it's nearly 10 o'clock. Carson's already in the studio. I'm surprised Denali let me sleep so late; I guess we kept him up late last night, too.

"Let me go potty, then I'll take you outside," I tell him as he nuzzles my neck and I scratch his belly. Never far from my side, he follows me into the bathroom, whining as I wash my hands. It's hours past his usual potty break, so I don't delay him any longer.

Every muscle aches as I descend the stairs, and my head hurts. Once outside, I take a seat on a patio chair as Denali does his business then runs to greet his friend, Snoopy, now on my lap.

Lately, I've busied myself in the office, spending less time with my canine friends.

"If you let me work, then I'll take you to the dog park later today." Both look to me while I speak, tilting their heads as if they understand my words.

I relax a few more minutes, watching the dogs explore the pool area and the grass beyond.

Fran knocks on the open office door, stating I should come eat some lunch. Glancing at the clock, I find it's two p.m. My body still aches as I pad my way to the kitchen. I spot both dogs lounging near the pool, so I eat my sandwich poolside today.

"Montana," Fran's voice calls to me.

My eyes blink, fighting off the bright sunlight.

"You fell asleep," Fran explains. "I don't want you to get a sunburn."

"What time is it?" I groan.

"It's after three," she states.

"Crap!" I sit up too fast, causing my head to spin. "I have work to do."

I bury my head in my work; time in the office flies. After a late dinner with the dogs, I take them for a long walk on the grounds and near the lake. It feels good to be outside. I love time with Denali and Snoopy. I really need to schedule breaks into my work days.

Carson

. . .

I call it quits at midnight. We've hit a wall and need the break. As I enter the house and make my way to our room, I hope Montana's still awake.

We've been working too many hours on the last two songs for the album. So much so that I can't remember if I saw her, outside of sleeping, yesterday or the day before. It's sad, really. We're newlyweds; we should spend more time together in and out of our bedroom. Unfortunately, for the past week, we've only been together while one of us sleeps. I keep saying, "One more day; one more long day." Then, we'll wrap up the album, and I'll devote entire days to her.

She left the nightlight on in the bathroom for me. I close the bedroom door as quietly as possible then tiptoe into the bath. Of course, Denali hears me. Tucked into Montana's back, his head follows me, but he remains quiet. I brush my teeth, strip out of my clothes, then slide into bed. I find myself jealous of the dog cuddled between us.

The next night, I'm sneaking into our bedroom long after midnight. Closing the bedroom door, I notice Denali is not in our bed; neither is Montana. Excitement grows as I walk toward the bathroom to find my wife.

"Montana," I murmur to her shadow lying on the bathroom floor, Denali's head on her back.

Denali whimpers.

"It's okay," I promise him as I squat down.

"Montana?" I shake her, but she doesn't respond. I roll her over, pulling her into my lap. She's pale as a ghost. She doesn't wake when I call her name a bit louder. Then, my body and brain snap into action. I pick her up and walk to the bedroom door.

"Help!" I scream into the hallway. "I need help!"

I snag a blanket off our bed, placing it over her in my arms.

The guys appear in my doorway.

"She won't wake up!" I speak quickly, unsure what to do. "Get Fran!"

Eli sprints toward the stairs.

"Did she take something?" Warner asks while Jake reaches out, his hand on her forehead.

"She feels normal, no fever," Jake states.

"I found her passed out near the toilet; there's vomit in her hair." As I speak, my eyes lock on Fran as she's entering the room.

She passes her phone to Eli." I've given the address; you answer their questions."

Fran looks to me then lays the back of her hands on each of Montana's cheeks. "She's had a flu bug for two days. No fever, but she barely eats or drinks. I put her to bed at nine tonight when I found her asleep in her office chair."

A flu bug. I didn't know. She's been sick for a few days, and I didn't know. Fran's words do calm me a bit. At least now I know it's the flu and not an overdose. *Thank you, Warner, for putting that thought in my head.*

After what seems like an hour, the EMTs arrive. While they take Montana's vitals, Fran shares her symptoms from the week.

"Is she on any medications?" the female EMT asks.

Fran looks at me, but I don't know. "I haven't seen her take any meds," I share.

When the next questions deal more with her family history, I decide I'd better call her mom. "Tony?"

"Carson, what's wrong?" Her frantic voice makes the weight in my stomach heavier.

"Montana's had the flu for two days," I explain, following the stretcher and three EMTs from our room. "I found her passed out by the toilet, and the EMTs need some information, okay?" It kills me every time the fact that I barely know my wife is pointed out. "I'll hand my phone to the EMT for you to answer their questions."

I descend the stairs, hearing the EMT speak to Montana's mom but not listening to a word of it. The sight of her loaded in the ambulance feels like a kick in the gut. My hands cover my abdomen. Fran pushes my back, urging me to ride in the ambulance with Montana.

When Tony joins us in the emergency department, Montana's still unconscious. I share the information Fran told me. In her motherly tone, she tries to calm my nerves.

I watch as the nurse replaces the empty IV bag with another. She promises Montana's improving with the fluids in her system.

Later, rustling near my head wakes me. I lift it from the bed, finding Montana looking down at me.

"Kiss... Beth..."

I barely make out her raspy whispers.

"What?" I ask.

Tony appears on the opposite bedside.

"Kiss..." Montana's eyes flutter closed. "B-e-t-h..."

And, she's out again. Neither Tony nor I understand what the two words mean. We attempt to work through it out loud, but we're too tired. The wall clock reads six a.m. We need Montana to wake; then, we need to go home and sleep.

Hours later, the nurse returns, taking Montana's vitals. At her movement and touch, Montana wakes again.

"There she is," the nurse says, greeting her sleeping patient. "How do you feel?"

"I... I'm okay," she croaks.

The nurse passes her some ice chips, instructing her to chew them slowly. After documenting on the chart, the nurse states a doctor will be in soon then leaves.

Tony swoops to her daughter's side, and I continue holding Montana's hand.

"What happened?" Montana asks.

"I found you passed out in the bathroom," I answer. "Fran says you've had the flu."

She nods, her hands quickly flying to the back of her head.

"You're dehydrated," Tony explains. "You'll have a headache until you rehydrate." She passes the cup of ice chips back to Montana. "You were mumbling about kissing Beth in your sleep."

"Hmm...?" Montana slowly tilts her head, her brow furrowed. "Oh. Not kissing Beth." She grins. "The song *Beth* by Kiss."

And? Was she dreaming about a Kiss concert?

She pats my forearm. "I now understand the lyrics," she states, her voice husky.

Damn. Just like that, she breaks my heart. Like the lyrics in the song, I've been working too much, making and breaking promises.

Tony interrupts my thoughts. "Well, now that you're awake, I need coffee," she states, approaching the door. "Carson, I'll bring you some, too."

A minute after Tony leaves, the doctor enters. "Hello, Mrs. Cavanaugh. I'm glad to see you alert," he says while reading her chart. "Gave us a bit of a scare, but both mom and baby are fine."

Wait. What?

"Nausea and vomiting are common in the first trimester," he continues. "I'll recommend some ways to prevent future bouts of dehydration. There are many reputable books on pregnancy with many helpful tips. Everything looks good here. I'll let the nurses know we're ready to discharge you." He looks from her to me. "Any questions?"

A million, I say to myself. He mentioned pregnancy more than once, so I didn't imagine it. *Did she even have the flu? Or was she just pregnant? Did she know? Did she know she was pregnant and just told Fran it was the flu? Why didn't she tell me? Surely, if she knew she was pregnant, she would tell me. Unless she's afraid to tell me. Is she afraid of how I might react?* I lean forward, elbows on my knees to start a dialogue, when Tony returns.

"Thanks," I mumble when she hands me a coffee.

Tony informs her daughter, "I met the nurse in the hallway. They're working on the paperwork to send you home."

While Montana looks shocked like me, her mother seems the same as she was an hour ago, tired and ready to leave. I look to my wife for guidance. She shakes her head once, eyes locked on mine. I assume we aren't sharing the news with Tony today.

"Will you be able to take us home?" I ask.

"Of course," Tony assures. "I wouldn't make either of you take a cab after the night we've had."

I would've called the band, not taken a taxi. *Shit! My phone's been turned off since I rode in the ambulance. The guys must be freaked out. I need to send them an update.* I ignore the text alerts; I know what they are asking. I tap on Eli's name.

> ME
>
> sorry
>
> phone off
>
> all better be home soon

36

CARSON

The Next Night

"About ready?" I murmur near Montana's ear, looking at our reflection in the mirror.

"Just a sec," she promises. "Are your parents here yet?"

I nod. "Fran said they arrived while we were napping."

Montana sighs audibly as her shoulders fall.

"You look perfect," I vow, kissing her cheek before turning her to face me.

"So far from perfect," she counters.

"You're perfect for me." When she scoffs, I relent. "Okay, in all honesty, you look like you've had the flu." I tell her what she already knows. "Most of them know you were sick. They'll be happy to see you awake and eating."

"Let's get this over with," she says before placing her lips to mine.

We hear loud conversations from the crowded front room as we make our way down the stairs, hand in hand. Noticing our arrival, the conversations dwindle.

"Let's eat," Montana suggests, swinging her arms toward the dining room.

Tony leans in close. "You look like you feel better," she says then continues with the crowd toward the table.

My father takes a seat at one end of the table while Montana's takes the other end. The rest of us line ourselves down each side. Peyton sits between Warner and Jake. Joe and Starr sit opposite them. Montana and I sit by them with Eli across from us. Tony says grace, and we fill our plates, passing food around family style.

Montana places a roll, some mashed potatoes, and a bit of chicken on her plate. It's not much, but it's more than she's been eating this week. I notice her mom keeps a close eye on her plate, too.

Montana and I make eye contact several times as we eat. Well, as I eat and she nibbles while around us, our family and friends converse on a variety of things, everything except last night's ER visit and the flu.

Montana leans into me. "Will you go ask Fran to join us?"

I do as I'm told, asking Fran to join us for a few minutes in the dining room. She argues until I tell her Montana wants to tell her something.

"Thank you for giving up your Friday night plans to join us tonight," I begin. "We have many things to celebrate tonight."

Montana takes my hand under the table. I nod my chin toward Warner.

"We officially finished our album last night." At Warner's announcement, everyone claps and cheers.

Montana nods to her brother, but he doesn't take the hint.

I rise. "Mom, Dad, we're glad you dropped everything to fly here today. We didn't want to worry you. The rest of us already know that Montana was in the ER last night. Well, early this morning, really." I look at my friends and family around the table. "I found her passed out on the bathroom floor from what we thought was the flu." I kiss Montana's hand in mine. "No need to worry about catching the flu bug tonight."

"Just don't drink the water," Montana giggles.

The guys look to each other in confusion. Peyton spews a mouthful of water across the table at us. Starr claps, and Tony tears up, a hand on her lips. After a few moments, I announce, "We're having a baby!"

Now, the table erupts with cheers and clapping. Pats on the back and words of congratulations surround us.

When we all calm down, Tony takes a turn. "Well, then it's settled. Kurt and Aaron, if you'll extend your stay, I'd like to throw a renewal of vows for Carson and Montana at our house. This way, the family may celebrate the marriage."

My parents agree to stay, and my mother offers to assist Tony with the preparations. I look to Montana to see if she's okay with the plans. When she smiles, I assume I need not shut down our mothers' plotting.

"And, I have one more announcement." Montana surprises me by standing. Again, she looks at Joe, and he's clueless. "As you're planning for Carson and I to renew our vows, I think you should know that another couple at this table should share their vows."

Understanding dawns on Joe's face, but Montana and I are the only ones to see it. Everyone else's eyes look to Peyton and the men beside her.

"Oh, hell no!" Peyton argues. "Stop looking at me; I didn't elope."

I have to laugh at her denial. Someday, she'll change her tune.

"Who?" Tony asks her daughter.

It's clear Tony's the only one who hasn't figured out her son and Starr are the ones.

"For Pete's sake, Mom." Montana points. "Joe and Starr were married in the African village before they flew home. Jeez." She sits down, frustrated.

I slide her water glass towards her hand, gently reminding her to sip often to avoid another ER visit.

Montana

. . .

Snuggled close, my head on Carson's chest, my mind rewinds the past 24 hours. What a day it turned out to be.

"Are you ready to talk about our news?" Carson asks, tucking hair behind my ear to reveal my eyes.

"What will I do while you go on tour?" I ask. "Stay in Des Moines or L.A.?"

"What do you want to do?" he asks.

"I don't know," I confess.

"Well, I'd prefer if you were with me in L.A. while we prep for the tour. Then, I'd love to have you on tour with me," he confesses.

"How would that work? Would I drive my own R.V. and follow your tour busses or be on the bus with you and all the guys?" I inquire.

Carson shrugs. "The guys have had women ride the bus with us from time to time. Most of theirs were one-night stands. But I'm sure we could lobby to sleep in the actual bed at the rear of the bus. The guys love you, and as long as you could tolerate all the smells that come with four guys crammed on a bus, it could work."

"I don't want to come between you and the band. I won't force myself where I'm not welcome," I state, tracing lazy circles on his abdomen.

"Do you feel welcome here in the house?" he asks.

"Yes," I answer honestly.

"See, the guys love you. It helps that you tease them back. It'll be hard for Warner to top the calf in his bedroom, but he will try," he chuckles, his hand rubbing my back. "We don't have to solve it all this week. I mean, we haven't even known you were pregnant for 24 hours yet. I have plenty of room in my house for us to start a family. Um, I'm getting ahead of myself. Do you like my beach house? We could sell it and buy another. Or, do you want us to live in Des Moines near your family?"

"You'd consider that?" I lift my head, resting my chin on my arm on his shoulder.

"Of course! I told you I'd really give us a chance. I don't care where I live."

I love this man.

37

CARSON

Sunday Evening

I hate seeing Montana like this. I understand her morning sickness messes with her all day long. On top of that, she's anxious about today's double wedding.

"Please relax and take two deep breaths," I urge as I pull into her parents' circle drive. "Remember, the doctor wants you to relax, because it's better for the baby. Besides, we've already had our real wedding; this one is pretend. You have nothing to be nervous about."

"It's not nerves," Montana states, tears welling in her eyes. "It's that my mother didn't approve our vows and the Las Vegas wedding."

"Please don't cry, honey." I rub my thumbs under each eye. "No one can take away our wedding. It was real, it was a spur of the moment, and it's ours."

Montana nods her head in agreement. I pull two pieces of paper from my shirt pocket. I open the first and pass it to her.

"Let's recite our own vows. These are the vows from our Vegas wedding."

"I can't believe you brought these," she chuckles. "I love you so much."

"So, we'll play along with your mom's wedding but recite our original vows." I open my door, hurrying over to help my wife and baby from the Jeep.

Montana

I lead Carson through the house into the backyard where I'm stunned silent. I blink my eyes several times to make sure I'm not imagining it. Sure enough, I'm standing on the patio in my mother's backyard, and it's not decorated with all things white and wedding. Instead, it's set up like it was for my birthday barbecue. The only difference is one white backdrop set up amid the greenery of her garden.

Mom *always* goes big. Her parties require hours of planning with decorations that match down to the napkins. Since Mom announced our vows for this weekend, I've dreaded her decorations and plans. I expected her to plan her vision of the perfect daughter's wedding. Even though she promised to keep it simple, I prepared for an over-the-top big ceremony.

"Everything okay?" Carson whispers, concerned as I stand here like a statue.

"She kept it simple," I whisper back.

Carson nods, lifting my hand to kiss it. I lean into him, thankful for his strength. He takes the paper gift bag from my hand, placing it on a nearby table, then guides me to a chair.

Our family walks over to greet us, commenting on my sundress and asking how the morning sickness is today. We visit for 15 minutes until Mom announces the minister arrives.

Carson helps me stand; I giggle. If he's this protective at four weeks, I can't imagine how he'll be when I'm the size of a bus with cankles and stretch marks and can't put on my own shoes.

Unraveled

Mom introduces Starr then Carson to the minister. She explains how we'll stand by the backdrop and states she'd like to take photos during the ceremony. All on the same page, we take our positions. Then, our family and friends gather around us.

As the minister speaks, a loud humming begins. I do my best to ignore it, but it buzzes overhead. Looking up, I spot a drone hovering above us. Annoyed, I return my attention to the minister. The persistent drone hovers lower, circling around Carson and me then the minister.

"Excuse me," I interrupt the minister. I can't take the incessant buzzing interrupting the ceremony. "Can we do something?"

"It's got to be the paparazzi," Eli states. "News of the ceremony must have leaked."

Suddenly, a loud thud sounds above us, and the drone splashes into the swim pool. We stand dumbfounded, watching the drone float.

"You're welcome," Peyton brags, hands on her hips. "Oh, Tony, I invited your neighbor over to join us as thanks for shooting down the drone for us."

I turn toward our neighbor's house, finding the boy proudly holding his tennis ball-shooting dog toy. He shot it at Peyton and me last summer as we lounged by the pool. I wave him over, thankful he took out the annoying drone.

"Carson," Peyton calls with her hand extended, "I need $100 to pay the neighbor kid."

Laughter fills the air.

EPILOGUE

Montana

With the album complete, the guys hang at the pool with Peyton and me during the day, and we entertain them in Des Moines at night.

Carson takes frequent calls from Meredith and the label regarding publicity for the album release and the upcoming tour. He calls a band meeting almost daily.

Using the tips found in the many pregnancy books Carson bought for me, I'm feeling better, and the morning sickness doesn't ruin my every waking hour.

News leaked to the press about his purchases; now, the paparazzi swarm and speculate that he knocked me up before the shotgun Las Vegas wedding. Peyton allows me to vent and helps me remember to ignore the headlines; she helps me focus on my life and not the rumors.

At the many band meetings, we've arranged for the Unraveled Tour to contain shows for two months, then take a month break, then repeat. With our baby due in mid-April, the tour takes a four-month break from

Unraveled

April to August, allowing the guys to be home. They brought me to tears when Eli suggested it, and Jake demanded the label give in to their planned breaks for the tour. These guys look out for me in every way.

We're in L.A. now. I work with Sonny and Matt to prepare the house for the baby while Carson and the guys practice on the stage for the tour. He's home each night for dinner, usually with at least one guy joining us.

Peyton and I video chat daily. She's running the Des Moines headquarters, complete with a full-time office manager and five warehouse employees. The influencers made our product a must have all across the U.S. Online sales skyrocketed, and retailers sought us out for the product. Carson's arranged for Peyton and me to meet our gymnast idol at the upcoming concert in Tennessee. I plan to fangirl hard; it will be embarrassing.

I have three new ideas for our next entrepreneurial venture, but they will need to wait until after the baby arrives. That gives me lots of time to brainstorm. I'm blessed to work with my best friend. Peyton refers to me as the talent of our operation.

Tomorrow, we will see the customized tour bus Carson and I will live on during the tour. The rest of the band will share another bus. Carson thought I deserved more privacy and a space of my own during our pregnancy. I think he wanted our own bedroom without three sets of ears listening nearby. Our own bus brings many advantages.

Each night, Carson sings songs from the new album to the baby. The sound of his voice often lulls me to sleep while causing the baby to kick. I don't have a favorite song; they're all about me. Carson poured his feelings into each one, further explaining the uniqueness of our chance meeting.

The first single released, *Unraveled*, currently boasts four weeks in the number one slot. *Undone, Before You,* and *Everything* slowly climb the charts, threatening to knock it off the top of the charts.

My summer began with a heavy decision on my shoulders—find a job or continue with college. Little did I know the whirlwind my life would become. Everything seems to fall into place, much to my surprise. I don't know what the future will bring, so I'm enjoying every minute with my family and the band.

When it comes to love, I'm lucky. Love at first sight really does exist.

The End
I hope you'll look for all 7 stories
in <u>7 Deadly Sins Series</u> of stand-alone books available now.
Help other readers find this book and give me a giant author hug—
please consider leaving a review on <u>Amazon</u>, <u>Goodreads</u>, Kobo, and <u>BookBub</u>—
a few words mean so much.
Social Media Links on following pages.

ALSO BY HALEY RHOADES

Ladies of the Links Series-

Ladies of Links #1 -- Gibson, Ladies of the Links #2 -- Christy, Ladies of the Links #3 – Brooks, Ladies of the Links #4 – Kirby, Ladies of the Links #5 -- Morgan

Boxers or Briefs

The Locals Series-

Tailgates & Truck Dates, Tailgates & Heartaches, Tailgates & First Dates, Tailgates & Twists of Fate

The 7 Deadly Sins Series-

Unbreakable, Unraveled, Unleashed,

Unexpected, Uncaged, Unmasked, Unhinged

Third Wheel

The Surrogate Series-

The Proposal, The Deed, The Confession

Trivia:

1. All character first and last names in this book are those of NFL Quarterbacks. (Except Denali & Snoopy the dogs)
2. The character Dawn is based on my best friend. During a car ride, I explained my next series of books and she suggested I have one random character that appears in each book. Thus, I named the character after her and awarded her Dawn's positive spirit. In 2015 she was diagnosed with stage IV colon cancer. They found it late and it had spread throughout her body. She had chemotherapy every two weeks for the next 8 years of her life. With all of this she was still a ray of sunshine and lifted others, like me, up. Her strength and selflessness inspire me to try and improve myself. She was the most upbeat and positive woman I know. I absolutely loved her laugh.
3. What are the seven deadly sins? The 7 deadly sins, also called 7 cardinal sins, are transgressions that are fatal to spiritual progress within Christian teachings. They include envy, gluttony, greed, anger or wrath, sloth, and pride. They are the converse of the 7 heavenly virtues.
4. Haley Rhoades is my pen name. I created it using 2 maiden names of my great-great-grandmothers on my father's side of our family.

ABOUT THE AUTHOR

Haley Rhoades's writing is another bucket-list item coming to fruition, just like meeting Stephen Tyler, Ozzie Smith, and skydiving. As she continues to write contemporary romance, she also writes sweet romance and young adult books under the name Brooklyn Bailey, as well as children's books under the name Gretchen Stephens. She plans to complete her remaining bucket-list items, including ghost-hunting, storm-chasing, and bungee jumping. She is a Netflix-binging, Converse-wearing, avidly-reading, traveling geek.

A team player, Haley thrived as her spouse's career moved the family of four, fifteen times to three states. One move occurred eleven days after a C-section. Now living the retirement life, with two adult sons, Haley copes with her empty nest by writing and spoiling Nala, her Pomsky. A fly on the wall might laugh as she talks aloud to her fur-baby all day long.

Haley's under five-foot, fun-size stature houses a full-size attitude. Her uber-competitiveness in all things entertains, frustrates, and challenges family and friends. Not one to shy away from a dare, she faces the consequences of a lost bet no matter the humiliation. Her fierce loyalty extends from family, to friends, to sports teams.

Haley's guilty pleasures are Lifetime and Hallmark movies. Her other loves include all things peanut butter, *Star Wars*, mathematics, and travel. Past day jobs vary tremendously from a radio-station DJ, to an elementary special-education para-professional, to a YMCA sports director, to a retail store accounting department, and finally a high school mathematics teacher.

Haley resides with her husband and fur-baby in the Des Moines area. This Missouri-born girl enjoys the diversity the Midwest offers.

Reach out on Facebook, Twitter, Instagram, or her website…she would love to connect with her readers.

- amazon.com/author/haleyrhoades
- goodreads.com/haleyrhoadesauthor
- bookbub.com/authors/haley-rhoades
- tiktok.com/@haleyrhoadesauthor
- instagram.com/haleyrhoadesauthor
- facebook.com/AuthorHaleyRhoades
- twitter.com/HaleyRhoadesBks
- pinterest.com/haleyrhoadesaut
- linkedin.com/in/haleyrhoadesauthor
- youtube.com/@haleyrhoadesbrooklynbaileyauth
- patreon.com/ginghamfrog

Made in the USA
Monee, IL
04 April 2024